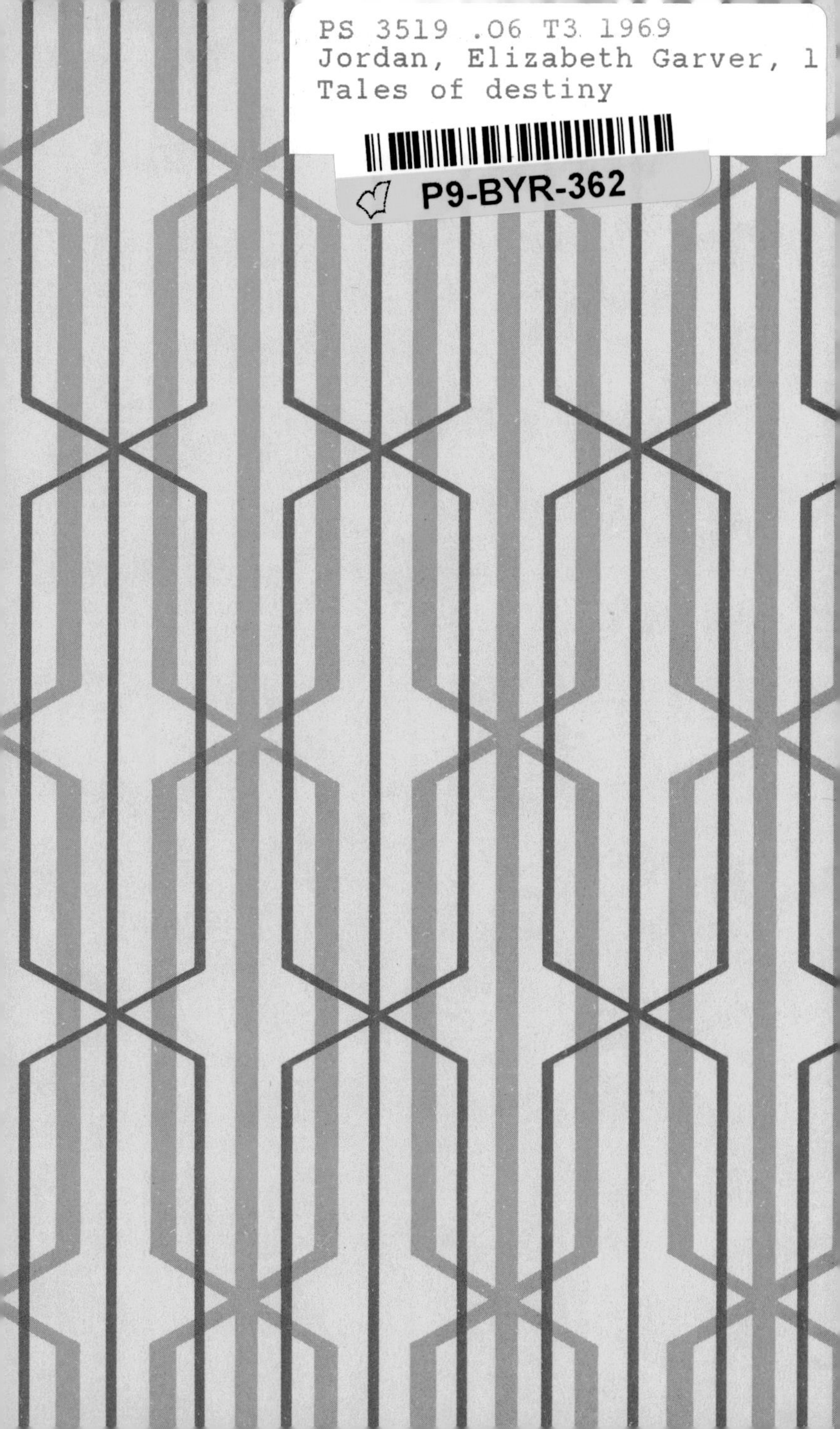
PS 3519 .O6 T3 1969
Jordan, Elizabeth Garver, 1
Tales of destiny
P9-BYR-362

Tales of Destiny

[See page 39

"SANG IT AS IF IT WERE A MERRY ROUNDELAY"

Tales of Destiny

by

Elizabeth Garver Jordan, 1867-1947.

Short Story Index Reprint Series

BOOKS FOR LIBRARIES PRESS
FREEPORT, NEW YORK

First Published 1902
Reprinted 1969

STANDARD BOOK NUMBER:
8369-3264-1

LIBRARY OF CONGRESS CATALOG CARD NUMBER:
79-103522

PRINTED IN THE UNITED STATES OF AMERICA

TO

MY SISTER ALICE

Contents

Illustrations

The Voice in the World of Pain

The Voice in the World of Pain

THEY had told her that only an operation could save her life, and that it must be performed at once.

The voice of the physician who first spoke seemed a trifle strained and unnatural as he delivered this decision. He hesitated perceptibly over his words, and his eyes moved restlessly as she fastened hers upon them. Even in the sudden mental panic that had seized her, and which she was controlling so well, she realized his discomfort and felt a vague gratitude for the sympathy that caused it.

It could not be easy, she reflected, to tell a young woman for whom life held as much as it did for her that a mortal disease had fastened on her. She who had always analyzed herself and others discovered that even at this crisis she was dreamily trying to follow the mental process of the famous surgeon who had begun to roam restlessly about the room.

"He will say nothing for a moment," she thought. "He is giving me time to pull myself together. I can, but I do need the time. He needs it, too. He has had to tell a woman who is young and rich, one who is ambitious and in love, something that may mean the loss of all these things. He has made her feel as if the world were slipping under her feet. The only thing that may save her—the knife. My work must stop, my friends must stand by helplessly. Even Jack can do nothing for me — dear Jack who would do anything—"

The objects in the room grew suddenly dim. She sank deeper into the big chair that held her, while despair, sudden and unreasoning, filled her soul. The question which has so often come to men and women in agony through all time rose in her. Why, oh, why, had existence begun at all, if it must end like this? To her the grim implacability of fate was as awful a revelation as if she were the only one to whom it had ever come. To be projected into the world through no volition of one's own, to be danced about like a puppet on a string, to have the body to which one is tied seized by disease, and to be forced to watch one's own decay, helpless to arrest or avert it—that was a horror before which the soul itself must shrink.

Her strong soul was appalled by the prospect. Many had leaned on it in the course of her young life, whose brightness had not made her heedless of the gloom in which some have to walk. Her strength had never failed them, but in this tragedy it was failing herself and she found no helper. She had made her appointment with the specialists and had come to them without a word even to those who were nearest to her. "Why should I go to them with my trouble?" she had asked herself. "It may not be what I fear, and I should alarm them unnecessarily. If it is—well, there will be time enough to tell them when I know myself."

She thought of them now—at least she thought of Jack. Was it only last June they had been married? It seemed as if they had always been together, as if they had always belonged to each other—as if life had only really begun when she met him. He came vividly before her, gay, debonair, his brown eyes full of the tenderness she knew so well. She pictured the change that would come in them when she told him. The thought wrung from her what her own suffering had not done. She groaned, and the three physicians at once assumed an air of professional interest.

In the interval of silence they had worn their usual calm. They were suave, polished, hopeful. In this atmosphere of cool, scientific interest the woman's will asserted itself, and she set her teeth with the determination to meet these men with a calmness equal to their own. She asked that the operation might be performed three days later, and found them thoroughly in accord with her wish to have the matter hastened. Every detail was arranged; the strain was lightened to the extent of a mild professional jest or two dropped with the friendly wish to convince her that the situation was not hopelessly tragic. Then she went to her carriage while three pairs of eyes looked after her and then at one another with an expression it was well she did not see. She directed the coachman to drive home, and, drawing her furs around her, gave herself again to reflection. Unconsciously she drooped forward a little in her seat, staring at the falling snow outside with eyes which hardly saw the streets and scenes through which she passed. At one point in the journey uptown the carriage was stopped for a moment by a sudden congestion of traffic; but she was not conscious of it. Her beautiful face, outlined against the dark collar of her fur coat and framed by the carriage window, drew the eyes of another woman who stood at the curb waiting for an opening in the line of vehicles. She, too, was miserable—but something in the expression of the eyes looking over her head made her forget her own burden in a sudden thrill of unselfish sympathy.

"Handsome and rich," she mused, as the line parted and she made her way across the street. "She seems to have everything; but her face—with that look of despair on it! She is wretched—more so than I am."

Nevertheless, she might have failed to recognize the face had she seen it three hours later when Mrs. Jack Imboden turned it towards the young Englishman whom her hostess of the evening had assigned to take her into dinner. She herself knew that she never had looked better, and Jack had confirmed this conviction when he folded her wrap about her as they were leaving home. She had told him nothing of the afternoon's experience; she could not, she discovered. There were limitations even to her courage. She could dress, she could meet a dinner engagement, she could look her best and be her brightest

—that much she could and would force herself to do. But tell Jack—no, not yet. The next morning, perhaps. If only he would have some business call to the West, as he had once had during the summer, and be detained until all was over—there was the germ of an idea in that. Perhaps, after all, she could arrange it so he need not know.

She was aroused from her reverie by the soft laughter of the young Englishman at her side. "This is delicious," he said, appreciatively, and she became conscious that she had been talking brightly, as usual, and that what she had just said was rather clever. Jack had caught it, too, and was looking at her with the expression she most loved to see in his eyes—a look of proud and tender proprietorship. Her own expression changed so suddenly that both men noticed it, and Effingham, the Englishman, commented upon it the next morning as he was giving an account of the dinner to his cousin.

"Mrs. Jack Imboden, who wrote that clever society novel last year, was in her best form," he said. "She got off some clever things, and told a good story that I'd tell you, old man, if I could remember how it went. But for all that, I don't believe she is happy. I can't explain it; but every now and then there was something—and once she looked at Imboden in the strangest way. She is too much of a thoroughbred to do that, you know, without good reason, and I rather fancied that something was up. Do you suppose they have quarrelled, or that he is not treating her right?"

His cousin, the Honorable Cuthbert Effingham, yawned widely. He had not met Mrs. Imboden, and the subject did not especially interest him.

"Since you've got religion, Albert," he drawled, "I've noticed in you a melancholy conviction that every soul but your own is unsaved and unsatisfied. Mrs. Imboden's all right. Perhaps her new gown didn't fit, or something. You're getting morbid. You won't even admit that I'm happy. Come with me and I'll give you my imitation of boyish glee over a game of billiards."

"The germ of an idea" evolved during the dinner that evening, developed well. By taking Jack's partner into her confidence, a rapid exchange of telegrams between the East and West made Mrs. Imboden's plan succeed so well that she drove with her husband to the station the day before the operation, and saw him whirled away in a westward-bound train. He had rebelled loudly over going; the subtle instinct that is the twin of perfect love had told him something was wrong. Once or twice she had almost faltered, almost confessed—it would have been so great a comfort to have him to lean upon. But she had sent him away, playing her part perfectly until the end. If, when the train rolled out of the station, she dropped the mask for a moment, there was no one who knew her to see it fall.

There was much to be done that last night—she thought of it, somehow, as the *last* night, absolutely. Her mental process refused to go beyond the events of the next day, and though she did not allow her thoughts to take on more than a hypothetical foreboding of death, she made her will, gave definite instructions to the friends who were now aware of what was to take place, and wrote a long letter to Jack which was to be mailed to him, "unless," as she put it to her maid, "within three days I myself give you instructions to the contrary."

The great surgeon came in the evening. He was deeply interested in the woman as well as in the case. He persuaded her to take a sleeping-draught, mixing it himself with a solicitude which would have surprised his colleagues had they seen it.

"You must sleep well to-night, you know," he said to her, "and you would not do it without this. You'd say you would, and you would try, but you would lie awake all night and think—which would be bad for you."

It was a long speech for the great surgeon. He himself was a little surprised, and was so still more when late that night he found himself giving his wife the history of the case. It was his rule not to carry professional matters into his home, and he was sorry he had broken it when he saw the tears his remarks called forth.

"You'll save her, won't you?" his wife whispered, clinging to him, and his answer was brief but full of feeling.

"She shall have the best I can give," he said, quietly; and the aroused womanly sympathy was content.

"I need not tell you to be brave," he said, looking down encouragingly at Mrs. Imboden the next day, a moment before the anæsthetic was administered. "You will be that, I know. But you must be hopeful. We are going to bring you through all right."

She smiled back at him faintly. "I will do all I can to help you," she said. "I will give you no trouble."

The saturated cone settled over her face, and the sweet fumes of the anæsthetic filled her nostrils and crept into her lungs.

"Take a deep breath," she heard a voice say. "Take a deep breath and count. Begin with one and count as long as you can."

She counted steadily to eight, drawing

in the fumes with each breath, and, unconsciously, breathing as little as possible. At nine a sudden panic came upon her. Her strong will broke and a sense of darkness and horror filled her. She opened her mouth to shriek, and a great, cold wave seemed to lift her and carry her away. She heard some one say, "twelve," "thirteen," "fourteen," and her heart was filled with pity for a wretched woman, who, far off in another world, was suffering. The words seemed to be forced by a tremendous will from a body in agony. "Seven-te-e-n," "eight-een," "n-i-ne-te-en," moaned the distant voice. Then all was blackness and oblivion.

When she again became conscious of her own identity she was one of a vast number of souls floating through a long, dark valley at the distant end of which gleamed a ray of light. She seemed, like the others, to be propelling herself towards this light with the dimly defined conception that it marked her objective point. But the journey was endless. Centuries seemed to pass, empires to rise and fall, worlds to appear and disappear as she travelled on. At first all was silence. Then the air was filled with a low moan, increasing in violence as she drew near the end of the valley, until it swelled to a vast diapason of human agony. Before the horror of it her brain reeled; she grasped blindly at the shadowy forms about her, but each swept on unswervingly. She felt herself falling, and as she sank the conviction settled upon her that this was at last the end. She did not know why, but she realized that if she lost her place in that dim procession she would never get back into the brightness of the world she was seeking.

Suddenly a voice, rich, soft, and musical, spoke beside her. It was a deep, strong barytone — a human voice. It rose and fell softly, persistently. She did not hear the words; but she knew at once that it was meant for her, that it was striving to reach her and to help her. To its humanity and sympathy she responded as a frightened child in the dark responds to the touch of its mother's hand. She felt strong, well poised, resolute. She found herself again a part of the throng around her, hurrying towards the light which grew brighter as they approached the exit from the valley. Through it all the voice remained beside her, uplifting and sustaining. As it grew stronger the whole valley seemed to her to be full of it, but the other shadows took no heed. The conviction strengthened that it was for her alone—that she alone heard it. A buoyant hope and strength took possession of her, and the appalling sense of loneliness departed. She floated calmly onward, out of the dense gloom into a gray twilight, then at last through the great arch at the end of the valley and into a broad, green field over which lay the blessed light of day.

As her eyes grew accustomed to the brightness around her she saw that the light came not from a sun, but from a brilliant dome arching over the field and from which radiated myriads of golden wires converging to a vast instrument in the centre. These wires threw out blinding and many-colored lights. At the instrument sat a woman of heroic size in flowing white robes that melted into the brilliance around her. Her great face was calm, beautiful, benign. On the greensward in front of her were thousands of men, women, and little children. Each was dressed in white, each face was distorted, and from each open mouth came cries of agony. From time to time the ranks parted, and one person was swept into the space directly before the instrument. The mighty hand of the woman sitting there struck a key, and as the note sounded one of the wires faded and the shrieking, foremost figure sank from sight.

Florence Imboden stood on the outskirts of the throng and looked at those near her, forgetting her own physical suffering in the sight of theirs. She seemed to understand at once what it all meant, and she accepted without question the explanation that suggested itself as one accepts the strange experiences that come in dreams.

"This is the World of Pain," she told herself, "and these are the souls of men and women whose tortured bodies are lying on operating-tables in our world below. The surgeons tell us when we come back that we have not suffered; but we do, we do!"

The young girl standing next to her was suddenly swept by some invisible force to the open space before the instrument. The woman left behind knew that her time was coming and braced herself to meet it. But fear, hideous, sickening, demoralizing, again claimed her. The head of the woman at the instrument bent to her, and she felt herself propelled forward. The pandemonium around her grew wilder. She realized now that the distant echo of it was what she had heard in her journey through the valley. She saw the mighty hand before her move towards the key, and her eyes followed it. The surface of the key was a transparent crystal. Looking through, she saw a room, bare, marble lined, with a table in the centre around which were grouped half a dozen white-robed figures. Four were men and two were women—nurses. On the table lay a figure. As she looked, the cone in the hand of one was lifted; a sudden stir of excitement was noticeable in the tense circle. Under the raised cone she saw her own face, white, still, terrible. There was a quick rush to and fro, the body was raised, something that looked like a galvanic battery was produced and used. The great surgeon turned from the table and threw up his hand in a gesture of hopelessness.

The mighty finger of the instrument moved implacably towards the key, shutting off the glimpse into the world below. She felt herself sinking, going, when again the wonderful voice that had sustained her sounded in her ear—melodious, golden, with musical inflections never heard in any other world, but never to be forgotten now. This time she could hear the words:

"Give her strength for the ordeal before her, and if it is Thy will restore her to the life in which she has done so much good, to the husband whom she has so greatly blessed. We ask it in the name—"

She raised her head without fear and looked into the calm eyes of the woman at the instrument. The voice went on. She heard the words no longer; but those to which she had listened were enough. She would live. She would live for Jack, "the husband whom she had so greatly blessed." Some benign, some powerful influence was behind her, strengthening and upholding her. She would live.

"She is coming round at last," said a voice, softly.

"That was a close call, doctor," said another. "I never saw a closer one. I was certain for a few seconds that the pulse—"

She opened her eyes. The white-walled room was whirling round her. Faces, vaguely familiar, appeared and disappeared. One, mistlike at first, gradually shaped itself into the features of the great surgeon. His stern eyes smiled at her.

"It's all over," he remarked, tersely. "Now you have only to get well."

"Doctor," she said, dreamily, "there is a soul—there *is* a soul. I have never felt certain of it before. And that voice—that wonderful voice that saved me—the voice that prayed. Where was it?"

She saw them smile a little at her seeming incoherence.

"Never mind, dear Mrs. Imboden, that's the ether," one of the nurses said, gently. But she persisted and questioned until the surgeon himself came to her bedside.

"Who prayed," she asked. "Who was it that prayed?"

He laid lightly on hers the steady hand that had worked so well for her, and spoke to her as one speaks to a fretful child.

"Now, Mrs. Imboden," he said, soothingly, "you must be very quiet. Don't talk. Don't think. As for this voice of yours—there has been no praying here." He drew on his gloves as he added, with professional pride, "We have been working."

She regained strength rapidly and some of her old-time brightness and buoyancy came with it. But when the news of the accident in which Jack Imboden had met his death was flashed to his New York home, they kept it from her as long as they dared. Before this double tragedy in her life her friends succumbed in silent despair. There was none among them strong enough to tell her, so they delayed while she talked of him constantly and counted the days that must pass before he could return to her.

When they finally told her, she turned her face to the wall without comment and asked them to leave her alone. Through the weary days and nights that followed she lay there making no outcry, no complaint; accepting what was done for her without question, silent, tense, automatic.

"She's losing strength every hour," said the day nurse, uneasily, to one of her associates. "This has destroyed her only chance. They shouldn't have told her—and yet how could they help it? She was constantly asking for him, and the anxiety and suspense would have been as bad as the truth. Her courage would have pulled her through—but this ends it. She will not have to mourn her husband long."

As the weeks passed, the same conviction came to Florence Imboden, like a flash of light across a midnight sky. After all—what matter? It would not be long.

In any case she might not have lived more than a year or two, and if that were so the situation was as Jack himself would have wished it to be. He would have felt that he could not live without her — now she need not live on without him. It was well. Only a short time and they would be together. *But would they?* The question loomed suddenly before her, black, forbidding, shutting out the light that had entered her soul.

Would they? Was there a hereafter? Was the soul immortal — or was death merely the sinking of the mortal into that nothing which is poetically called eternal peace and sleep?

In her full, bright life she had never before had these questions come home to her. She had attended church, she had freely given from the abundance that was hers, she had felt deep respect for the aims and teachings of religion and for the conviction of her religious friends. But in her soul she was conscious that she did not *know*—that she had never been convinced —that religion was not the vital thing to her it was to some others. Now her heart cried out for faith, for conviction, for immortality.

"If I could be certain of meeting Jack again," she breathed, "how cheerfully, how gladly I could bear whatever comes."

She recalled the firm conviction in which she had come back to life after her operation. "There is a soul, there is a soul," she had told the doctors, with her mind full of that experience in the upper world, her ears still hearing the tones of that marvellous voice. They had smiled over her words, telling her the episode was merely an ether vision and a common one at that. No doubt they were right, she told herself. The shock of Jack's death had pulled her down from any spiritual heights she might have reached to the earthly plane on which her only need was the sound of his voice, the touch of his hand. The mysterious voice had haunted her for a few days. She had thought of it, dreamed of it—but now that, too, was gone. She was getting out of touch with every human thing — worse than that, with every spiritual thing. This, at last, was agony. What had gone before was nothing. She was alone, hideously alone. She had called on God and heard no answer. She tried to pray and the prayers seemed a hollow mockery. She sank into lethargic despair.

Effingham found her so one day when he had begged to see her for a moment. It was the first time they had met since her illness, as he had unexpectedly sailed for England the day after her operation was performed. She had always liked the sympathetic, clean-souled, ascetic young Englishman, and she found herself speaking to him as she had spoken to no one else.

"You believe in a hereafter, do you not?" she asked, wistfully, while he was studying, with a sense of shock, the great changes in her.

He flushed a little, with the Englishman's disinclination to touch upon the subjects most sacred to him. But something in her eyes and face made him respond simply and fully.

"Dear Mrs. Imboden," he said, "I do, indeed. The faith I have in God and heaven is very near to me. You know," he added, slowly, "I am preparing for the Church, and I am here to study with a dear friend who has helped me more than any one I have ever known. If you have doubts—if you are looking for strength and conviction, he can help you, I am sure. He is a wonderful man. Will you let me bring him to you, or, better still, will you go with me to his church some day? It is not very far up-town, and I would like to have you see him among his people. Just now he is giving a series of afternoon talks: every one of them is an inspiration. Perhaps," he added, "you would be willing to drive up there with me now."

She hesitated. "I have gone out but a few times," she said, doubtfully. "I am perfectly able to go, but it seems so hard for me to move—to rouse myself from the condition of lethargy I am in."

The tone and her expression made Effingham unusually persistent.

"Come," he urged. "We'll sit at the

back of the church, and nobody will see us. You need not see Livingston afterwards unless you wish, although I fancy you will want to talk to him when you have heard him. People usually do."

She allowed herself to be persuaded, and they drove up-town together to the little church, tucked modestly out of the way in an unfashionable side street. The winter day was drawing to a close, and the church was but dimly lighted. As they entered a pew near the door they saw that all the seats were filled by shadowy figures leaning forward as if in prayer. They settled themselves comfortably and gave themselves up to the quiet and peace of the place. Through the door at the right of the sanctuary a man came. She could see his figure but dimly in the uncertain light. He stood for a moment looking over the assembly and then began to speak.

At the first word, Florence Imboden started to her feet. The voice was a deep barytone, full of musical inflections, heard by her but once before—but not to be mistaken when heard again. It was the voice of the World of Pain—the voice that had comforted, the voice that had saved. She buried her face in her hands while her brain reeled. Her mind was going at last, she thought; no mind could stand the accumulated horrors of these last few months. She tried to think calmly. It was the voice—but the other had been only "an ether vision." Had they not told her so? This man was strange to her—but that voice was not—could never be. She tried to pray but could not. A nervous tremor convulsed her. She rose and groped her way out of the pew. Effingham, suddenly roused from his absorption, assisted her without question into the street where her carriage stood waiting. She motioned the footman away.

"I want the air," she said to Effingham. "Let us walk up and down for a few moments."

They strolled along the deserted street, the young Englishman supporting her with friendly sympathy. He did not speak at first, but as he saw her grow calmer he broke the silence.

"I am afraid you did not like him," he said, with some disappointment; "and I am so sorry. I felt sure he could help you."

She made no reply, and he went on talking with the friendly purpose of giving her time to collect herself.

"He has helped me, as I have told you, more than any one else, and I have perfect confidence in him. I turn to him not only with my own troubles, but with those of my friends. I hope you won't mind my telling you," he went on, a little diffidently, "that I took yours to him. When I learned of your — your illness, I went to him the day before sailing and asked him to pray for you during the operation, which was to be performed the next afternoon at two. Before I had been in England a week I had a letter from him.

"He wrote that your case strongly appealed to him—had 'taken hold of' him, as he put it. So much so, in fact, he said, that he had knelt down in his study and prayed for you tor two hours while your operation was going on. Why, Mrs. Imboden—"

She reeled slightly, but his strong arm held her up. Her mind was not going, after all; it grasped as much of the strange experience as she could understand. She did not know why it should have come to her of all the world, but she did not question, either. It was for some great purpose, she felt. When the human soul was taxed beyond its powers something divine entered in and helped it. She was no mere atom whirling through space, to exist for a little time and perish. Back of the mystery of life was some benign power—she did not know what, but she was satisfied. In these dark hours of her life it had given her this proof that it existed. She could safely trust herself to it. She looked up into Effingham's eyes with a sudden light in hers which gladdened him.

"Your friend can help me," she said, "and he shall—more than any one else in the whole world. He shall teach me and I will believe—I know it. Let us go to him now."

The people were coming out of the little church as they turned back together.

They stood aside for a moment to let the others pass. Off in the darkness the street-lamps began to twinkle; above, the crescent of the moon hung pale in the twilight. Florence Imboden drew a deep breath as she looked up at it. The tragedy of life, of which her mind had been so full—what was it? Nothing. Fear, pain, loneliness, all these were swept away by the mental illumination that had come to her. The grim spectre of death itself was a benign friend, waiting smilingly beside her. Her prayers were answered. It was well with her—it was to be well with her. No matter what came, or how long or short the time, she could bear, she could wait. This little life was not the end. There was another world, another existence—complete, perfect. She did not know where, but it was somewhere—and in it—Jack was waiting!

An Episode at Mrs. Kirkpatrick's

An Episode at Mrs. Kirkpatrick's

FROM the first the new-comer did not appeal to the other boarders at Mrs. Kirkpatrick's select establishment. There were various reasons for this. She was, to begin with, very diffident and rather plain. The close observer might have seen beauty in her face, and the student of human nature would have liked the character shown in the poise of her head and in the direct glance of her brown eyes. But there were few close observers at Mrs. Kirkpatrick's table, and fewer students of human nature. They were busy men and women, slightly imbittered, perhaps, by boarding-house meals, and by abortive efforts at hospitality within the confines of one room. They observed that the new-comer did not contribute to the persiflage that served as conversation at meal-time, and they decided that she was dull. When they discovered that she had taken a hall bedroom and moved a piano into it as an auxiliary to her efforts to master the art of singing, their indifference gave way in several instances to acute disapproval, and the young woman whose room was next to the singer's sought the landlady with an energetic protest.

The landlady soothed her, as she soothed all the worms that turned. It was doubtful, she said, whether Miss Dixon would remain long. Yes, Dixon was her name—Helen Dixon—and her home was in some little town up in Pennsylvania. The girl had come to New York as an experiment, with a small amount of money she had "saved up" by teaching school. She could remain only as long as this money lasted; but she thought she had a voice, and that it needed cultivation. Mrs. Kirkpatrick did not agree with her in this theory, and her own voice dropped mysteriously as she added her suspicion that the experiment would be a brief one.

"An' I guess you won't be troubled much when she is singin'," she ended, cheerfully. "She's got a poor little peep of a voice that can't creep through the key-hole. I don't think she'll find many teachers in New York to encourage her."

Mrs. Kirkpatrick was wrong. Miss Dixon had no difficulty in finding a teacher—a young man recommended by the organist in her native town, and sadly in need of pupils. He accepted a large portion of the girl's savings as advance payment, and the lessons began.

Several days later it dawned upon the members of Mrs. Kirkpatrick's "family" that they had among them a source of inexhaustible hilarity. It was Miss Dixon's voice, and it was always with them. They heard it when they left the house in the morning, and when they returned at night; and it never failed to greet them as they came to luncheon or dinner. It was in the air the livelong day—a feeble, plaintive thread of voice, chirping like a depressed sparrow under the eaves, sometimes running on scales and exercises, again pitched high on ambitious operatic efforts, but ever and always off the key.

The inmates of Mrs. Kirkpatrick's house, being humorists, did not observe that it was plaintive. When they discovered that Miss Dixon took herself very seriously indeed, the situation developed in humorous charm, and when she finally began to talk shyly about her "art," which was at the beginning of her fourth week of study, they gave themselves up to unrestrained joy, and to a secret and corporate understanding from which she alone was shut out.

Meal-time actually became popular at Mrs. Kirkpatrick's. There had been a "once" when her boarders permitted themselves to be lured away by other attractions, but this was past. Now they assembled gladly around the festive board, and the subject discussed there was music, and the favorite authority on that topic was Miss Helen Dixon, assisted by her admiring associates. She remained serenely unconscious of the pleasantry that went on at her expense, and when they urged her to sing for them, as they did, she accommodated as many as she could in her room, in which the folding-bed curled modestly up against the wall, and the remainder of her guests sat in the hall outside and clasped each other's hands in ecstasy. She sang a great deal of operatic music for them, and there was one simple song, only one, which she deigned to attempt—"The Land o' the Leal." She pitched this very high, sang it as if it were rather a merry roundelay, and in a key not even on speaking acquaintance with that in which the accompaniment was played; so it made a delightful evening's entertainment, and was greatly appreciated by her guests. She used to accept their thanks with a shy smile and a really pretty blush; and once or twice, under much urging, she repeated to them encouraging tributes from her "master," a gentleman who seemed to share their sense of humor, for he allowed her to choose her own music, and assured her that she was making gratifying progress.

At the end of her second month she began to appear only at breakfast and dinner, omitting luncheon on the ground that it interfered with practice, and by the middle of the third month she was dispensing with breakfast also, substituting milk and a roll in her room. It looked as if she might soon lead a foodless life—through practice. Mrs. Kirkpatrick admitted that the girl had made a new arrangement with her by which she paid only for her room and her dinner, thus saving the remainder of her money for lessons.

"Of course I don't do that often," she added, "but she is so dead set on it, and I suppose it won't do her any harm. She gets one good meal a day, anyhow." Mrs. Kirkpatrick was good-natured and philosophical.

Under some conditions it might possibly have occurred to Miss Dixon's fellow-boarders that at this point her position had ceased to be unrelievedly funny. But habit is a great power, and she had been amusing them for three months. Moreover, just at this time she caught a cold, which, while it did not seem to be serious, added an especially grotesque quality to her voice. It did not seem necessary to her to cease singing for the benefit of her inflamed vocal cords, so she continued the usual evening concerts, and on one of these occasions the enjoyment of a certain young man was so intense and unclouded that it gave birth to suspicion in Miss Dixon's mind. She wheeled on the piano-stool and faced her audience with a long, direct gaze. They took it variously—some, like the unfortunate youth, with most primitive shame, others with ill-cloaked confusion, one or two with a muttered apology—but on each face lay revealed the story of deception. Miss Dixon rose, opened the door, and stood for one instant facing them. Then, with a gesture surprisingly full of dignity, she indicated the small hallway which, to her mind, stood for the wide outer universe.

"Will you please go—all of you?" she

said. "I see I have been—amusing you this winter. I am sorry I did not understand, but—where I came from—people are different—"

It was not a florid rebuke, and there was no elocution about it, but there was an unsought dramatic touch in the manner in which she suddenly sank into a chair, rested her head on the back of it, and burst into tears. Her cold and the lack of food had perhaps weakened her—but to those who left her there and went slowly downstairs she seemed very strong in that weakness. They had not meant to be cruel; they were merely shallow and foolish, and because they were they did not know how to show the real contrition that now disturbed them. They stood around aimlessly in the hall for a while, before drifting away, and as the days passed they sought to catch her eye, and to beam upon her, and to say genuinely friendly things. She remained very quiet and unresponsive. She still practised, but much less than formerly, and never in the evenings; and she was at the table now so seldom that she had been ill for several days before they missed her and dared to ask each other where she was. The landlady told them, rather shortly. The doctor had talked about pneumonia, and "she was sure she didn't know what she'd do if the girl got sick!" It was useless to send for her mother, who was old and delicate.

Boarding-houses are like prisons in that vital things are occultly communicated. The boarders grasped at the opportunity for reparation, and the women said eagerly that they would nurse Miss Dixon, taking turns by day and night, if she would allow them that privilege. A committee of two, whose deeper shame did duty as a welling sympathy, waited on her with this request, and even to their untrained eyes the utter collapse of the girl was evident. She thanked them listlessly, but showed an entire indifference to her situation. Apparently it was a matter of no importance to her whether she was nursed or not. She turned her face to the wall and sank into a singular condition of stupor, over which the doctor frowned reflectingly when he came again that night.

Just once, during the days that followed, she roused from her lethargy, and this was when a young girl in the neighborhood, also a musical student, who had met her once or twice, came in to make a sisterly call. Miss Dixon suddenly opened her eyes and asked the visitor to sing, repeating the demand several times with strange persistence and energy. She wanted "The Land o' the Leal," and the other sang it softly, but very sweetly, in a sympathetic mezzo voice, suited to the simple pathos of the words and melody. At the end Miss Dixon thanked her. "Somehow," she said, drowsily, "I seem to understand it better than I ever did before." She dozed again, and through the evening and the long night the women who watched beside her heard her repeating some of the words softly to herself, over and over:

> "I'm wearing awa', Jean,
> Like snow in the tha', Jean,"

and for the first time it came home to them, as it had seemingly already been borne in upon her, that this was true—that she was "wearing awa'"—that she had long been "wearing awa'" before they noticed it, and that she might not get well.

The next morning they sent for her mother, and the doctor came twice during the day, and over the establishment of Mrs. Kirkpatrick there rested a heavy gloom. The men were able to go off and divert their minds. The women who were at home, and on day duty in the sick-room, went about with reddened eyelids and with aching hearts. It was late in the afternoon when she turned upon them the direct glance of her brown eyes, which seemed suddenly wide awake and brilliantly expressive.

"When my mother comes," she gasped, "be good to her. And don't tell her—don't tell her"—her face twisted strangely as she struggled for utterance—"don't tell her you laughed at me. Don't—let—her—know—I failed!" In that gasping prayer lay for two women both the punishment and the lesson of a lifetime. For she spoke no more. At long intervals a few words of the old song passed her lips, and during the night she moaned wearily once or twice. Towards morning she threw her arms up over her head with a long sigh of utter exhaustion, and lay very still—and over the room settled the great solemnity and the peace Death brings with him when he comes. The watchers, who had never been so near him before, felt his presence before they turned to the bed from which the soul of Helen Dixon had passed, leaving there a most unhumorous little dead woman who smiled up at them inscrutably.

That odd smile still rested on her lips when her mother came, and the delicate old woman who was led into the dark room seemed to find in it the comfort of a message and a promise. For hours she sat there, holding the hand of her dead child, her one child, and to her came the kind friends who had done so much for her Helen. She knew, she said, for Helen had written home during the winter of their friendliness and their sympathy with her work. Now she wished them to tell her of her daughter's last weeks. The letters had been less frequent, and a little depressed, she thought; no doubt it was this illness coming on. Would they tell her all—everything?—no detail was too trivial for a mother's ear and a mother's lonely heart—

The brave old voice trembled slightly, but she conquered the human spasm, and faced her visitors with a quaint, old-fashioned dignity of manner. One by one they talked to her there and told her all—all that they had planned to tell her after her daughter's dying charge.

It was of the girl's voice they spoke most—of its beauty and its promise! They told her what it had been to them to know her daughter and to enjoy her singing, and to watch her delight in the art she was studying with such gratifying results. It was not subtle lying that a diplomat could have admired, but it was convincing to the one hearer. They said no one of them had ever heard a more sympathetic voice, and they repeated enthusiastic comments of her teacher, and finished with a little tribute from a musical critic brought forward for the occasion. As they talked the woman bowed at her daughter's side, straightened herself, and held her white head erect, and almost forgot for a few seconds that her daughter's voice was hushed forever.

"Then she *was* happy," she breathed. "She was happy the last winter of her life! I sometimes feared—she had had so many disappointments, so much grief. And towards the last her letters— But you all loved her, and you were kind to her, and she was happy—she was happy—oh, thank God—thank God for that!"

She laid her head on the silent breast of her child, and cried softly, but they were not bitter tears; and as she wept it seemed to the women sitting there as if the smile on the cold face against the pillow became ironical—but that was perhaps because they were tired, over-strained, and—knew it should be very ironical.

They carried out with unfaltering mendacity their plan of atonement, and what they lacked in *finesse* they made up in human pity and zeal. They had Miss Dixon's teacher call on her mother the next morning, and the young man did his part simply and naturally, and told his dim-eyed listener of the career her child might have had, if she had lived. Then he did something which would not have occurred for one moment to his artless mind save for the conversation he had the night before with Miss Dixon's fellow-boarders.

"I want to ask a very great favor of you," he said, a little huskily. "Miss Dixon had just paid me in advance for another quarter, and that money, of course, would in any event be returned without question. I would not trouble you with such a detail at such a time, but I wish also—very much—to return to you all she has paid me this winter. It—it was enough payment to have her as a pupil." With which masterly lie he laid the little packet on the table, and stood up, looking with boyish and genuine sorrow at the white head below the level of his broad shoulders. A sudden thought of his own mother came to him, and he gulped hard as he said good-bye, and went away.

In her place by her daughter's side Mrs. Dixon talked that afternoon to Mrs. Kirkpatrick.

"So much kindness, so much sympathy," she said. "Oh, how it has helped to know that my poor darling had such friends! They knew her so short a time, and yet they loved her so. But it was always that way with Helen; she won hearts easily. In our town every one loved her; they have always come to her with their troubles—the children and the young girls, and even the older women. She was the teacher so long, you see—and she was so good to them. Strangely enough, they were not interested in her music, and they tried to discourage her from going to New York. Several times she had money saved to come, and she gave it to friends who were in trouble. My neighbors would say to me often after she finally came, 'Well, Mrs. Dixon, if Helen has found friends half as good to her as she is to others, she is fortunate.' And I was glad to be able to tell them that she had."

The little woman rambled on, and Mrs. Kirkpatrick moved restlessly in her chair. She had not been oblivious to the situation in her house that winter; she firmly reminded herself now that she had taken no part in it, and that, on the whole, she had been considerate towards the girl. The situation seemed to call for some reassuring reflections.

That afternoon there came to the house from the little town in Pennsylvania a silent, dark-browed man who quietly and capably took charge of the Dixons, living and dead. The mother burst into wild weeping when she saw him, but later she confided to Mrs. Kirkpatrick how supreme was the relief of his presence.

"He told me he would come," she said. "but I was afraid he could not get away. He is almost like a son to me—is Jean—and I would have liked him as a son. He has always cared for Helen, since they were children together. But she did not love him that way, so they were just friends. I've always been sorry she didn't marry him, and I hoped perhaps she would, some day, when I left her. But she has gone from me first, and I am alone—"

The simple services were held that evening in the tiny room of the dead girl—and because it was so tiny there were present only the mother and Jean and the clergyman, which was as it should have been. Mrs. Kirkpatrick's ample proportions overflowed across the lintel of the door into the hall, and back of her were members of "the family," unhappy and strangely ill at ease in the presence of Jean Mackenzie. Then, as the exigencies of boarding-house sensitiveness require consideration, the other painful details were attended to late at night. At half-past eleven a sombre vehicle stood in front of Mrs. Kirkpatrick's house, and grouped about it in attitudes of patient waiting were the driver and the undertaker's two assistants, who were to go with it to the midnight train. In the drawing-room the mother waited for the precious burden to be carried down-stairs;

"'YOU'VE KILLED THAT GIRL AMONG YOU! YOU KNOW IT, AND I KNOW IT'"

above, Jean Mackenzie turned his sombre eyes on the men and women of the household who had assembled in the little upper hall.

"I'm not going through the farce of thanking you people for what you've done," he said. "You've tried to make up for it these last few days, and you've managed to spare her mother. She'll thank you—the dear old soul! But you've killed that girl among you! You know it, and I know it. She wrote me the whole story —and God knows I tried to get her away from you. I tried to make her come back home where people knew her for what she was — the sweetest, gentlest woman that ever lived—tender beyond words to everybody and everything. It was that kind of woman you chose to guy to death. No wonder she didn't see it; no wonder she didn't understand. How could she when there wasn't an atom of meanness and cruelty in her beautiful nature. And to think she did not let us know when she was ill! To think she had to die here among you—*you*—"

The door of the bedroom opened softly, and the men came out with their burden. Gently they bore it past the group and down the three flights of stairs to the hearse which awaited it. The street was dark and silent; there was no one near as the plain casket was slid into its resting-place and the door was snapped shut. The undertaker's men climbed to their places beside the driver, and the horses started off at a slow walk, their iron-shod hoofs falling with a harsh, metallic click on the asphalt pavement.

A single carriage drew up at the curb, and Mr. Mackenzie gave his arm to the little mother in the drawing-room, and tenderly led her forth. At the door she paused and looked once more around the circle of pale faces which a strange fascination had drawn together for this last scene. She kissed the women.

"How can I thank you?" she sobbed. "How can I ever thank you?"

The hand of the man beside her tightened on her arm.

"Come, mother," he said; "I have thanked them for you."

He helped her down the steps, put her in the carriage, and took his place beside her without a backward look.

"Helen's friends," they heard her sob, as the driver lifted the reins. "Such good friends to my poor little girl."

The carriage moved off slowly through the deserted street, following Helen Dixon on her journey home to the people who loved her. The group of men and women on Mrs. Kirkpatrick's front steps looked after it with straining eyes until it turned the corner. They were a silent and a downcast group, in which a too exuberant sense of humor had been blighted at its fullest flower as by a heavy frost.

The Wife of a Hero

The Wife of a Hero

WHEN Sergeant Ralston, of the —th United States Infantry, received his commission before the outbreak of the Spanish-American war, the enlisted men of the regiment rejoiced exceedingly and the officers without exception gave him a cordial welcome to their ranks. Ralston was not only an excellent soldier, but a very popular one. There was something singularly magnetic in his personality. He was the handsomest man in the regiment and its crack athlete; but he remained wholly unspoiled by success and an amount of praise and attention enough to have turned any young head. He was wholesome, loyal, sincere, and unassuming. He worked indefatigably, but never lacked time to serve a friend. Radiating health and happiness as the sun does warmth, he was yet the one to whom his associates instinctively turned in times of sickness or trouble. He was a paragon, in brief, about whom, in the entire course of his military career, but one unkind remark had been made. That emanated from Major Buckstone, a confirmed dyspeptic, who had long contemplated with gloomy eyes the joyous existence of the young sergeant. He once said, tersely, that young Ralston would be endurable if he had a redeeming vice — a comment over which Ralston himself smiled with utter simplicity.

When the young man became lieutenant and a more interesting object than ever in his new uniform, the officers promptly admitted him to their club, while their wives began no less promptly to speculate as to what manner of woman Mrs. Ralston might be. He had left the post the week after he received his commission, and had returned a fortnight later with a bride of whom nothing was known save that she was a very beautiful woman. Ralston adapted himself to his new position with an easy grace which left nothing to be desired, though it stimulated a mildly wondering speculation as to his past. His wife, however, might be wholly different—"quite impossible," as the Colonel's wife apprehensively put it when she was considering the matter in council with her friends. It was finally decided to invite the Ralstons only to the large social functions of the post—such as receptions and balls. On these occasions a critical eye could be kept on Mrs. Ralston, and if she conducted herself fitly the glorious possibilities of more exclusive affairs would lie open to her.

It was an excellent solution of the problem, which doubtless would have met every requirement had it been carried out. But just at this juncture war was declared, and, before the women of the post had recovered from the shock, the regiment was ordered to the front. There was joy among the men and grief among their wives. There was a tumult of expectation, preparation, and excitement. Then the regiment marched away with band playing, colors flying, and hearts under the new uniforms beating less gayly than they would have but for the heavy hearts left behind.

Mrs. Ralston was at the station to see the last of her handsome husband, and even in their grief many of the women observed her. They saw that she was young and lovely, with a Madonna-like beauty that touched the heart appealingly; saw, too, that she was suffering and bearing her suffering with a dignity equal to their own. Several of the older women, steeled by experience in Indian campaigns on the frontier, mentally resolved that they must and would do something for her. They had each other to lean on—and she was utterly alone. But they forgot her as they watched the crowded train bearing away their own to sickness, to battle, perhaps to death. To each woman there was that day just one man in the world—not especially striking or heroic to the casual glance, but already a laurel-crowned hero to the wet eyes that strained for a last look at him.

Mrs. Ralston was turning away when the Colonel's wife touched her lightly on the arm. The two looked at each other. For a moment neither could speak. Both faces were wet with tears—tears that had not fallen until the last car rounded that distant curve. The appealing brown eyes of the young lieutenant's wife gazed pitifully into the motherly gray ones of Colonel Holman's "commanding officer," as he called her, and in that instant there was born an affection and an understanding between the two which helped them both through the weary months that followed.

For a time it was not so hard. The regiment was comfortably camped at Tampa, and glowing reports came back of the excellent condition of men and officers. May days in Florida were not unpleasant, they discovered, and the active exercise and out-door life kept them in good health and high spirits. The women left behind at the post sewed, read the newspapers, wrote long letters to their absent lords, and became acquainted with Mrs. Ralston —something last in fact but not in importance. Mrs. Holman, who did nothing by halves, took up energetically the wife of the young lieutenant. There were no social functions in progress; but the two rode and drove and sewed together, read each other extracts from the letters written by their husbands (Ralston's epistolary style was as charming as himself, the Colonel's wife discovered), and the bond of friendship between the two grew stronger as the weeks rolled on.

The other women followed the example set them, for no one could long resist Mrs. Ralston. She was so sweet, so charming, so unconscious of her striking beauty, so warmly sympathetic and so modestly responsive to each friendly advance that she slipped without effort into the very heart of the exclusive circle and found a loving welcome there. When they discovered that she had a beautiful contralto voice and sang with art as well as feeling, her little triumph was complete; but she remained as unconscious and as unspoiled as her husband. The Ralstons were much alike—so alike that Mrs. Buckstone voted such even sweetness open to distrust. As this sentiment was regarded as a wifely plagiarism, it fell rather flat. Mrs. Ralston sang to them, banished their headaches by the soothing touch of a woman's magnetic hand, raised their drooping spirits by her own bright hopefulness, thought of and did a thousand little things that soothed any fretful forebodings of theirs, without a thought of sympathy for herself from any one. She wrote something of it all to her husband in the field, whose fond and proud replies were not among the extracts read to Mrs. Holman.

Then came the sailing of the transports for Cuba, and anxious days at the post until it was known that the regiment was landed safely on Cuban soil. News, more or less accurate, filled the extra editions of the newspapers. The —th Infantry, under Colonel Holman, was to take part in the attack on Santiago—that much, at least, was definitely known by the women at the post. They read the defences of the intrenched Spanish army, they absorbed the surmises of gifted journalists as to the plans of attack, they followed with sick hearts the accounts of the weary marches and the bitter hardships of their husbands, sons, and brothers. Then came the days of waiting when both armies were lined up face to face, like blood-hounds in leash, awaiting the signal to fly at each other's throats.

The great battle was to begin at sunrise the next morning. Then on the day following that. As a matter of fact it had already begun and was raging at that moment with great loss of life among the Americans. These conflicting reports flooded the country in the extra editions of the newspapers, for heartaches must not interfere with circulation. Hour after hour dejected army women pored over them with eyes that saw only blood-stained battle-fields and stricken, helpless figures lying uncared for in the long grass.

There were few open moans among these women—that would have seemed beneath the dignity of brave officers' wives. They merely kept out of sight, away from the sympathetic questioning of friends, and bore the agony of apprehension as best they could, in dignity if in despair. Mrs. Ralston alone was buoyant and hopeful.

"They will come home full of glory and triumph," she said to Mrs. Holman. "Your husband will be a brigadier. Everybody will be a hero, and the regiment will parade through the streets while the city goes mad with patriotic joy. I feel it —I know. If it were to be otherwise, some instinct would tell me."

Mrs. Holman took the younger woman's face between her hands and kissed it lightly on the cheeks.

"My dear," she said, "in that remark you show your artless innocence. From your adaptability to all things here I had fancied you knew more about army life. If you really think that glory follows valor and that anything but a pull will bring promotions you are a dear little baby in your knowledge of us." From which comment it will be seen that Mrs. Holman was in a depressed and bitter frame of mind.

In the field Lieutenant Ralston was no less sanguine than his hopeful young wife. Through the terrible days when the army was marching towards Santiago he was, as ever, the life and inspiration of the regiment. His superb physique seemed to defy illness and fatigue. He was always cheerful, always hopeful, always stimulatingly gay. A few of the men who had withstood his fetching ways up to this time succumbed to them now. Ralston's name ran through the letters home as the love motif runs through Wagnerian opera. Ralston had nursed this one; he had "braced up" that one; he had divided his last suit of flannels with another who had recklessly thrown his knapsack away during the weary march. Ralston was "a thoroughbred," "a trump," "a corking good fellow," so ran the enthusiastic tributes from enlisted men and officers alike. When they reached the post these eulogies were passed on to the young officer's wife, who proudly thanked God for them and for him, and felt how much she had to live up to.

When the day of the fight dawned and the regiment made its historic charge up San Juan Hill, no one went into the action more blithely, more gallantly, than Ralston. The men of his company loved their captain, but adored their second lieutenant. It was Ralston's yellow head to which their eyes turned, his flashing eye to which their courage responded. They saw them both for a time as the regiment began its bloody climb up the slope. Slowly the men crept forward, the death-song of the Mauser bullets on every side, the crash of artillery in the distance, the moans of dying men at their very feet. Death ploughed many furrows in their ranks, but men dashed forward to fill up the gaps, and the blue lines crawled irresistibly on. Far up the slope they saw Colonel Holman, his left hand whirling his sword awkwardly above his white head as his right arm hung broken at his side, while his hoarse-voice orders boomed above the roar of the fight. An electric thrill of pride ran through the regiment at the sight, and the men cheered wildly.

Ralston, his virgin sword gripped tightly in his hand, heard the cheer, and wondered what had gone wrong in him that he felt its force so dully. He kept his place, climbing slowly up the hill with his company against the enemy's fire, but a strange, indescribably horrible sensation was settling upon him. Was he hurt? He had thought so at first, for the feeling had numbed him so suddenly. A moment ago he had been laughing at his men. The next, the space at his right and left, where two eager comrades had been pressing forward against his shoulders, was suddenly made void as two limp bodies fell with grotesque abruptness at his very feet—dead things, that but this moment had been men. The hand that was so tightly grasping his sword began to tremble. An unseen force seemed to clutch his throat. He felt giddy, and a deathly nausea seized him. There—another man in front had gone, and another just behind him. His captain had fallen early in the action, and the first lieutenant was in command of the company. At last he, too, was down—on his knees first, dying hard, with spasmodic effort to rise, his hand reaching for the sword that had fallen beside him, his tongue calling a last order to his men—a hero thrust out of the world through glory's wide portal.

Ralston's place was forward. It was his to lead. The men in the company were looking at him, with a new lust for blood in their eyes, their faces distorted by the savage wish to bring swift retribution to the enemy for the loss of their officers.

Nothing could hold them back; it was Ralston's place, his envied privilege, to lead them on amid that deadly hail-storm of shrapnel and bullets.

It was his duty, he told himself dully, but he could not move. His feet seemed nailed to the earth. His tongue felt paralyzed; he could not utter an order. His brain was numb. The next bullet would hit him, he reflected, and he, too, would be a dead thing, trampled upon by comrades hurrying to the front. The Spaniards were aiming at the American officers, that was evident. They fired at men who carried swords and had stripes on their trousers. He would be the next victim—or was he in some horrible nightmare from which he might mercifully awaken before his mind went? No, it was no dream. He was in the great fight of the nineteenth century—a fight that would go down in history. He was there—an officer in the American army—placed by the death of his superiors in command of his company. They were waiting for him to lead them; already the human lines were wavering a little, and on the familiar faces near him he saw settling a look of doubting comprehension and horrent consternation. They saw what was the matter. Well, let them see. He could not lead them. He knew he was afraid. He branded himself a cursed coward as he tottered on his trembling limbs, then fell full length on the trampled grass. With a yelp of mingled rage and loathing his men swept on, in glad obedience to the leadership of Sergeant O'Grady, who had promptly grasped his opportunity.

How long he lay there he did not know. One in extreme mental agony takes little heed of the flight of time. At first he thought only of himself—his young, boyish self, so full of life and the joy of living, and so soon to be swept out of the sweetness and beauty of it all into the coldness and darkness of some Cuban grave. His teeth chattered, a tremor shook his powerful figure. Then his mind turned to her—his wife, the woman he so loved, the woman who tried to love God as much as she loved him. At this very hour she was sitting in their far-off home, unconscious of his peril, unconscious of his—

The thought seared his soul like a red-hot iron. Unconscious? Yes, thank God for that! Unconscious that he had failed—that he had turned his back on comrades and country in the supreme moment. He groaned aloud. But it was not too late even yet. Already the strange numbness was leaving him, already the blood was beginning to stir again in his veins. He would follow his company, he would fight, fight, fight! He would wipe out with blood, his own if necessary, the memory of that damning syncope of the coward's panic. He would up and follow his comrades, and some day he could look into her dear eyes again.

His yellow head, lying like a cluster of flowers in the dusty, trampled grass, caught the eye of a Spanish sharp-shooter in a distant tree. He grinned as he took aim; the man doubtless was wounded, but it was so easy and such pleasure to end the whole business with that yellow target gleaming there invitingly. The willing bullet sang on its way. There was a convulsive leap of the powerful figure on the grass, a silence, a stiffening. The golden head, red now and matted from the swiftly flowing blood, turned a little, then buried itself more deeply in the dusty soil. The sharp-shooter watched it closely, then turned to other prey with a smile of satisfaction. He knew the signs. Another American officer was out of the fight—out of all fights for all time, unless, perhaps, somewhere one who has failed here is given another chance.

The desperately fighting regiment pushed doggedly on, the rear companies working like demons to follow their comrades to that hill-top. Men and officers recognized the recumbent figure, the fair head resting in the dark pool that told the story. Even in the tigerish excitement of the hour a lump came into many a throat at the sight, and it stung to added fury these men who had not seen the prologue which made it so much more a tragedy than they dreamed. To them the beloved young officer had died as an American soldier should, fighting bravely with his face to the foe. Some of them turned aside for a momen't, carried the limp figure to a more sheltered place, covered the distorted face and the blood-dappled, curly head, and rushed back into the fight with set teeth and one more score to settle.

It was these men whom the newspaper correspondents saw that night after the sun had gone down over the hill where so many of the —th Infantry lay dead and dying. And so, in the brief and inaccurate reports, sent with infinite difficulty to the great American dailies, the name of Ralston stood out in a way to demand the largest type the editors could select to do honor to the hero dead. Ralston was only one of the many brave men who had fallen that day, but he was the idol of his regiment—not only a hero, but one who lent bravery a new charm by the insouciance of a courage which was magnificent in itself — Ralston, the gay, the blithe, the debonair. He had figured in preliminary despatches that told of his strength, his athletic prowess, his influence over the men. All the newspapers had his photograph "in stock," and the first page of every "extra" showed his winning face, smiling sunnily within the black border with which the editors had decorously framed it.

By the time the enlightened correspondents were able to send correct reports, Ralston was enshrined in the hearts of his countrymen as a hero. The meagre despatches from the front had been skilfully padded in the home offices of the newspapers. The most brilliant writers of the staff had been bidden to exercise their imaginations and utmost style on this fascinating subject, so full of "tears" and "human interest." In the editorial columns, too, there were lengthy tributes to Ralston, "the brilliant and strikingly handsome young officer who lies dead on Cuban soil, but whose magnificent bravery in action has stirred the pulse of all America."

At the post, anxious-eyed women whose husbands lay wounded in the field hospitals turned from the contemplation of their own trouble to read those extracts to Mrs. Ralston. At first she had not been able to bear them. She had gone down before the blow of her husband's death as a prairie-flower sinks under a bronco's heel. But as the days went on and she began to realize that the heart of her country was yearning over her in her sorrow, she roused from her stunned apathy and sought to demean herself as behooves a hero's wife.

It was not easy. Glory is not a full offset for happiness in gentle souls. She had never been well, notwithstanding her cheery assumption of health; but she prayed for strength to go through what was left of life as Herbert would have her go. She would live for others, do for others, as he had done. She would make herself worthy of him—of this magnificent being who had been given to the world for a little to teach her the meaning of happiness, and to show men how to live and how to die.

She went among the women of the post, calming the frantic fears of the wives of enlisted men, nursing the sick, caring for the babies, tiding over for every one the bitter days and nights of waiting for official lists of dead and wounded. The slender figure, which grew pathetically thinner from day to day, went in its black gown "along the line," bringing comfort and peace in its wake. Even the assertive lamentations of Mrs. O'Grady learned modesty in the presence of the brave woman who was bearing her great grief so admirably. But something in her expression disturbed these friends, slightly skilled as they were in analyzing expressions of the human countenance. She looked "like an angel," as Mrs. O'Grady said, but her color was too feverishly crimson, her eyes too brilliant, not to cause anxiety in those who loved her. Every one did, by this time—so much that when at last the long-looked-for letters came and the truth about Ralston's death lay coiled in them, there was a hurried conference at the post and a decision prompt and general.

"She must never know," said Mrs. Holman, with nervous emphasis. "Colonel Holman writes me that the correspondents have decided to keep the matter quiet, and we must do it, too. If she were to find it out the shock would kill her. Her heart, the doctor says, is very delicate. All that sustains her is the thought of the courage—God help us!—with which he died. When the regiment comes home she may be stronger, and perhaps, even then, it may be possible to keep it from her. None of the men will tell."

It was not hard to keep it from her. She was so unsuspecting, so secure in her great pride and faith. If her friends at the post talked less of him, she talked more. She would not have his deeds forgotten so soon while she had a tongue to voice them. The slight constraint with which her words were met seemed to her a little touch of envy, perhaps felt on account of some brave fighter whose record had not met so prompt and complete a recognition. And so she talked to Sergeant O'Grady's wife, and the Irishwoman listened with bent head and wet eyes, and replied with the tact and sympathy which women of higher caste could scarce have bettered. It was not easy to have Mike deprived of any particle of his share of honor — but Mrs. Ralston was speaking, and Mrs. Ralston was the terribly widowed charge of the post.

The situation when the regiment came home in September was a difficult one. But the men were warned by their wives, and the honest, gallant fellows consented to keep the secret. She was the bravest of the brave. Why kill her because her husband was a coward? They had dumped Ralston without ceremony into as hastily made and as shallow a grave as bare humanity would permit. It was not easy to give a dramatic story of the burial, but they did it somehow, though they could not meet the eyes of the widow as they told it to her. As the days passed, however, and they saw the results of her ministrations at the post and heard of her unselfish efforts to help their wives and families, they improved in their irksome rôle of lesser comrades of a dead hero. Mrs. Ralston wanted the detailed account of every look, every word, every act of Herbert's, and they gave it to her with what generous mendacity they could command.

In this reminiscence of the earlier days at the front, even the bitterness against Ralston himself began to die out. It could not live in the face of his widow's beautiful love and trust, and among the thoughts of the time when he had been so dear to them all. Perhaps it had been insanity—poor, earth-born servant of charity! But the delicate shoots of pity and regret for him, that began to push up through the crust of contempt which had formed about his memory, were chilled by a sudden frost. President McKinley announced that the bodies of American soldiers would be brought home in all cases where their families wished this to be done. Mrs. Ralston was one of the first to act upon the permission. Herbert should lie among his people, be laid in his glorious grave with all the honors to which his rank and heroic death entitled him.

The decision created consternation at the post. Men who had until now aided the kindly deception, announced firmly to their wives that here they drew the line. Sergeant O'Grady was especially intolerant on this point. His disgust drove him to deep potations. The result of this effort to quiet his desire to protest was that he called on Mrs. Ralston with the purpose of opening her eyes a little. He did.

He stumbled home afterwards with but

little understanding of what he had done. When morning had brought sobriety and reflection he tried with a sick heart to recall the interview. He could not, beyond a general conception of a kind of nightmare in which two terrified brown eyes stared at him out of the darkness. One thing she said penetrated even his numbed intelligence, and he told it to his wife in the depth of his contrition.

"I do not doubt your word, sergeant," she had said. "You are an honest and a brave man, notwithstanding the condition you are in to-day, and I know you would never have said this unless you thought it true. But if the whole regiment, the entire American army, told me so in chorus, I would not believe them any more than I do you. There is something behind it all that we do not understand—something which some day"—her voice for the first time broke a little—"my husband will explain to me."

Mrs. O'Grady repeated this to Mrs. Holman the next morning as the two stood together looking at Mrs. Ralston. The

Irishwoman had gone to her after the sergeant's conjugal confession, to make such explanations and apologies as she could. She had found her sitting at her desk, fully dressed, her cold fingers grasping the pen with which she had begun a letter to the President. She had been dead many hours. Heart disease, the doctor said, and he added with wise gravity that probably death had been caused by some sudden shock. If that were true, there was no evidence of it in the beautiful face at which Mrs. Holman looked through bitter tears when she came in answer to their agitated summons. Death had come to Mrs. Ralston with tender courtesy and she had received him with a smile — so serene, so sweet a smile, that one look at it was to know that all was well with her.

It checked Mrs. Holman's tears. She bent and kissed with twitching lips the parting in the soft, dark hair.

"She died because she could not hear her hero wronged," she said, sadly. "Now that she is with him—look at that smile! He may be her hero still."

Victoria Delsaro, Missing

Victoria Delsaro, Missing

MISS VICTORIA DELSARO was wont to remark in moments of extreme bitterness that in the length and breadth of Manhattan there was no one so persistently and unscrupulously made use of by friends and acquaintances as herself.

It was natural that this reflection should occur to her. Being a young and not especially attractive woman, with two million dollars and no incumbrances, she was regarded as a source of income by a surprisingly large number of persons. In the beginning, when she had attained her majority and her fortune, and her guardian had stepped aside with a suave farewell and a few words of conventional but well-meant advice, she had rather enjoyed the rôle of Lady Bountiful which was immediately assigned her. She was naturally generous, and she liked to make people happy. Her desire had full scope, and two or three very busy, rather educative, and distinctly expensive years had passed before she began to analyze the effect of lavish giving on the subjects of her bounty and herself. Several "disappointments" had, of course, been sufficiently deep to demand her attention, but she had waived these lightly enough, and had refused to consider them as having any bearing on her future actions. Still, when disappointments ceased to be conspicuous because they became the rule rather than the exception, the thoughtful mind of Miss Delsaro, surprisingly mature even then, took up the problem this fact presented, and considered it while she went on in her chosen course.

Gratitude, she decided, was a sensation that had no home in the breasts of her protégés. Not even the stimulating expectation of coming favors developed a present sense of appreciation. She discovered—very slowly, for all this was a matter of years and evolution — that it was considered almost a kindness to her to permit her to occupy her mind with and expend some of her great wealth on "worthy objects."

"It is a fad with her, you see," one of her dear girls had explained, in cheerful ignorance of the fact that Miss Delsaro was within hearing. "She likes to find clever people and get the credit of their training and future success. When I go into opera, of course she'll boast that she discovered me, sent me abroad, and paid my expenses, but"—this very magnanimously—"I shall not mind."

Miss Delsaro did not mind, either, in this case, for the refreshing egotism of youth and talent was back of it. The girl was at least studying and profiting by her advantages, which could not be said of all of Miss Delsaro's "finds." She learned to give with good-natured indifference to the absence of gratitude, finding her reward in other results, and in the fact that she was presenting to the world many artists and singers whose talents, but for her, might have perished obscurely. She was, she knew, not alone in her experience, but her comparative youth, her freedom from all restraint, and her great wealth made her, as she said, "a chronic victim of the undeserving poor."

It was natural that after five or six years of this she should learn to look with somewhat jaundiced eyes upon a greedy world. It was perhaps natural, too, that when greed had in several instances manifested itself acutely within the circle of her closest friends, she should magnify the importance of the incidents and necessarily conclude that here, too, lay coiled the serpent of guile. Nevertheless, she was at heart a sane woman, with a well-balanced mind and an inheritance of common-sense from her eminently practical and successful father. She might have forgiven and forgotten the friends who had so skilfully used her for their own purposes, had not the One Man appeared precisely at this juncture and furnished her with the final and pitiless lesson fate intended her to learn.

The One Man was singularly attractive. His handsome eyes had a merry twinkle as he looked at life's play, and he found special favor in the eyes of Miss Delsaro. She liked his optimistic point of view, his lack of the tact and suave policy of other men in her circle, his apparent indifference to wealth, society, and high places.

"He is merely a great big happy boy," she reflected, as she watched him play tennis one afternoon at the Country Club. He had hurled himself into the game with the zest of a school-boy, and his crisp, fair curls were damp from the energy of his play. Under his small mustache his white teeth flashed as he smiled at his opponent, and his movements were as light and graceful as those of a trained athlete. Victoria Delsaro studied the picture with a satisfaction she conscientiously strove to analyze.

"He is merely a boy," she thought again; "thirty-four years of life have not made him a man, and thirty-four more will not do it. He is as irresponsible and as care-free as a fawn. His income is large enough to live on comfortably, and he will never add to it by a penny earned. He cultivates the people he likes, shuns the people he doesn't like, no matter what they could do for him in a worldly way, pursues pleasure, carefully avoids pain, is supremely selfish and absolutely honest—the darling!"

The last words flew from her brain to her lips, but no one heard them—not even the One Man, who suddenly presented himself before her, wiping his damp brow, and blithely indifferent to the informality of his attire.

"May I drive home with you after I've gotten into things, and have some tea?" he asked, eagerly. "I've something I want to tell you."

Miss Delsaro gave him a smile which proved that something pleasant can happen to a dark and rather heavy face. She felt the weight of her thirty-six years drop from her under the influence of his radiant youth.

"Can you be ready in twenty minutes?" she asked. "I am to take Mrs. Allen home, and she is leaving at five."

He assured her that he could. "I'll be dressed in ten," he laughed. "And then I shall come out here and sit around and say things in your hearing about women who delay men with important matters on their minds."

He hurried away as he spoke. Miss Delsaro rose from her place among the spectators and wandered leisurely across the grounds and up the steps leading to the cool veranda of the Country Club. She told herself that she would send some one in search of her coachman. In reality, as she well knew, she longed to sit in a cool, deserted corner and think, and smile inanely to herself with no one near to see it. For Miss Delsaro was in love!

She was recalling every look and feature of the One Man when steps echoed round the corner of the veranda, chairs scraped the floor, and the voices of two men reached her. They had taken seats out of sight, but unfortunately not out of hearing. She knew the voices well.

"So Harrington's going into the new trust, too, is he?" asked the first voice. It belonged to the stout and wholly amiable president of the club.

Miss Delsaro unconsciously pricked up her ears. Harrington was the One Man.

"Yes," said the second voice, that of Tompkins, the multi-millionaire. "He wants to come in, but we're not going into that for our health, and I told him it would cost him a cool half-million. He knows it's the chance of his life, and he'll take it, with Miss Delsaro thrown in. She'll accept him at the drop of the hat—every one knows that—and as the deal doesn't go through till fall he can get her to cash up in time."

The president moved restlessly in his chair.

"I didn't suppose he cared for her," he said, slowly. "I imagined he didn't care for anybody, the selfish young pup."

There was an instant of silence. While it endured, Victoria Delsaro pictured to herself very accurately the look of supreme scorn the financier turned on the president, and the length of time before he spoke showed he got the full enjoyment of letting it sink in.

"Harrington wants the money," he said, dryly. "I thought I mentioned that. He's very ambitious under that irresponsible, play-boy jollity of his."

Miss Delsaro did not wait for the president's reply, nor did she draw her breath too sharply. She walked quite with her wonted air into the club-house, gave her order to a servant, and descended the steps when her carriage arrived, her dark head high and an enigmatic expression in her eyes. Harrington was waiting, and Mrs. Allen was not far off. She motioned to them rather curtly. Mrs. Allen took her place with a depressing sense that one of Victoria's moods was also a guest of the day. Harrington, sitting in front, wheeled half round and poured forth a cheery monologue. If he observed Miss Delsaro's reticence at all, he ascribed it to natural modesty over the coming interview.

They deposited the relieved Mrs. Allen before her own mansion and went on. On Harrington's smooth face a slight shadow was gathering—a reflection, perhaps, of the heavy cloud resting on his lady's brow. It was growing late. Before them a declining sun was painting the water and the sky in tones of gold and crimson.

"Wouldn't you like to walk?" asked Harrington, suddenly. "Why not let the coachman go on, and we can follow slowly and enjoy that." He indicated with a wave of his hand the gorgeous panorama before them.

Miss Delsaro gave the order. "Better have the farce over," she decided, "than prolong this agony of anticipation."

Harrington scrutinized her curiously as they fell into step.

"You look," he said, "as if somebody had offended you. I hope it is not I. If I have, it is the bitter irony of fate. For I came with you to-night to ask the greatest of favors. I want everything from your hands—I want you."

Under the circumstances, it was badly put. Miss Delsaro turned white.

"And the half-million?" she asked, harshly. "That, I understand, may wait until fall."

He stopped sharply, faced her, and looked into her eyes for a long minute. She returned the gaze steadily, showing in her own eyes the scorn she felt.

"Some enemy of mine—" he began.

"Oh no," she said, lightly, "a friend—your future partner, in fact. Mr. Tompkins confided all your hopes and prospects to Mr. Hamilton on the club veranda this afternoon, and I necessarily overheard him. He did not know that, or he might have shown a more delicate reserve."

Harrington lifted his head, resumed his place by her side and walked on.

"When you interrupted me," he said, "I was about to add an explanation to my proposal. I was going to say that I don't amount to much—which I need not say now, in view of your recent discovery. But I am not a mere fortune-hunter. I have some money of my own; quite a good deal. If you had married me you would not have had to support me. I should certainly have asked you for that half-million, but you know Tompkins, and you must realize how safe and good an investment it would have been. It would have made me a rich man, and, so to speak, in your class. You would have lost nothing. I love no other woman. There is no woman in the world who has a claim on me—and I was offering you a good name and a clean record. I think," he added, naïvely, "we should have been very comfortable together."

Miss Delsaro's severe brows formed a straight line.

"I disagree with you," she said, briefly. "If you consider that you have proposed, you may consider that I have refused."

There seemed to be nothing more to say, and Harrington walked on beside her in a depressed silence. The coachman, full of a lively appreciation of the situation as he conceived it, had driven rapidly and was out of sight. There was a constrained parting at the entrance of Miss Delsaro's country house.

The next day she went back to town, engaged a suite of rooms in a Fifth Avenue hotel, and gave out that she was soon going abroad.

"What I should like to do," she confided to her one confidante, a delightfully worldly but unspoiled spinster of forty—"what I should like to do is to drop absolutely out of sight for a year or two. If I could, I would disappear to-morrow and begin a new life in a new land and under a new name."

Miss Van Dorn laughed quietly.

"Too sensational," she said, tersely. "The yellow journals would trace you to the other side of the world, and the Sunday after the discovery they'd have page pictures in red, green, and purple, showing you trying to jump off the earth's surface. Really, you'll have to give it up, dear."

She looked at her friend with real sympathy as she spoke. In her mind there was a shrewd conjecture as to the reason for this sudden restlessness.

Victoria Delsaro said no more, but the

words she had spoken carelessly and without thought had in them the germ of an idea which grew. It was one of her fads to carry a large amount of money in a small bag she wore around her neck.

"One can never tell when my friends may need it," she had said, ironically. Now she began to add to this fund. In the back of her brain there lurked the thought, never again expressed, that some day she would step on a train for San Francisco, and sail from California to the Orient without the idle ceremony of farewells.

"They'll say I'm crazy," she reflected, "but I cannot fancy anything on earth that is of less importance to me than what they say."

Her subconscious thoughts were running in this channel one afternoon as she walked up Fifth Avenue to her hotel. At Fortieth Street she became vaguely aware of the presence of a crowd, and, self-absorbed though she was, she felt the tense excitement of men and women who surged past her, bent apparently towards one objective point. Farther up the avenue a yellow flame leaped into the sky, and at the same moment the shrill, warning scream of fire-engines rang in her ears. Close upon the echo of this came the tumult of the approaching trucks and the wild hoof-beats of flying horses. Men and women took refuge on the steps leading to residences, in their efforts to avoid the horses driven to the curb and on the sidewalks by excited drivers striving to make way for the engines. Miss Delsaro fell back with the rest against the inhospitable stone.

"It's the Winfield Hotel," she heard a man cry. "It's burning down, and hundreds of people in it are burning to death."

The clang of ambulance bells lent a dread emphasis to the statement. Swinging round the corners from east and west came the frenzied horses, lashed by their drivers, while trim surgeons in spotless white duck uniforms made hurried preparations for patients. Miss Delsaro looked on, sick at heart, and with straining eyes. Her hotel was burning down — her acquaintances in it were perhaps among the victims. She tried to move forward, but her trembling legs refused to carry her, and the rapidly increasing crowd held her a prisoner. To go farther up the avenue was impossible. She succeeded in pushing her way back to the corner, and forcing a path through the crowd in the side streets. She was terribly excited. Strange noises rang in her ears, and she felt herself shivering. She had a childlike longing for the sound of a familiar voice, for the touch of a friendly hand. Instinctively she directed her steps towards Miss Van Dorn's home, only a few blocks away. Suddenly a thought flashed into her mind as vivid in its impression as if it had been written and held before her eyes. For one moment she hesitated. Then, with a characteristically quick movement of decision, she walked over to Third Avenue and Forty-second Street and took an elevated train for South Ferry.

One week later Miss Delsaro, tucked in a steamer-chair and cosily wrapped in rugs by an attentive steward, watched the California coast recede into the distance as the great liner cut its way towards Yokohama.

The rush of departure and the numerous small details needing her attention had so occupied her mind that in all those seven days she had not really faced the fact of the exceedingly vital step she had taken. She had not looked at a newspaper until she reached San Francisco; then she had read with entire calmness her own name among the long list of victims of the Hotel Winfield fire. There had been a good deal of "fine writing" on the subject of the dead heiress and much speculation as to the division of her great fortune, for she had no relatives, and, so far as was known, had left no will. Miss Delsaro postponed the reading of these details until she was safely away from America. She had experienced, during those last days in her native land, almost the sensation of an outlaw fleeing from justice. She was desperately afraid of being caught! Without too much thought or secrecy she had, in a way, disguised herself. She scorned any facial change, but few would have recognized the elegant Miss Delsaro in the very plainly dressed and rather dumpy woman who went on board the *City of Peking* just before it sailed. She had arranged her hair in a severely simple fashion, and her gowns were of the ready-to-wear variety. She might have been a companion or governess going to the other side of the world to join her employers. But rolled up among her rugs were several newspapers, full of the harrowing details of her last hours, whose scenes no one had witnessed but all had imagined, and it was these newspapers Miss Delsaro unfolded before the California coast was two hours behind her. The cool audacity of the act would carry it, she reflected. No one would see in her the dead heiress to millions. She must take chances in this enterprise. If she were recognized, her plans must fall through. If not, it would be another proof that the gods were with her in her new life.

Nevertheless, as she read the journalistic accounts of the Winfield victims, strange sensations visited her soul. She herself, she read, had not been seen to leave the hotel the day of the fire. Her maid, the only servant with her at the hotel, had asked and secured leave of absence for the day, and had left the hotel early in the morning to visit relatives in New Jersey. Miss Delsaro was seen in her rooms after luncheon by a servant who answered her bell and delivered a note she gave him. Not one of her friends had seen her alive after that, but some one had seen her, he thought, at the window during the fire; and the next day, among the charred bones found in the ruins was a hand to which still clung a ring recognized as one Miss Delsaro often wore.

The heart of the woman in the steamer-chair contracted. She had given that ring, only the day before the fire, to Lettie Ormsbee, who lived with her mother in the hotel. They had been Miss Delsaro's best friends there, and she had loved the girl dearly. Both mother and daughter were among the dead. Dear little Lettie! Where was she? And she herself—Victoria Delsaro? Was this whole experience a horrible nightmare? It began to seem like one to the woman who had voluntarily given up identity and her place among the living. Her nerves, strained by the crowding episodes of the week, revolted fiercely. For an awful moment she doubted her sanity, her very existence. Back there lay her native land —the land she loved, for she was a loyal American. Back there, too, were wealth and luxury and many friends who loved her, and many others who needed her. She had forgotten them. She had given no thought, either, to those protégés of hers, helpless in distant lands if her bounty failed them. She had turned from all that was hers and from all she had been —for what? She tried to pull herself together and answer the question resolutely. For individuality, for freedom—for the privilege of living her life as she pleased and of being weighed by the standards of other men and women. She would drift round the world under the new name she had assumed, avoiding, for a time at least, the beaten paths of travel. She would study the men and women who made up the average of humanity, and she would find friends among them. She would earn her living when her money gave out and it became necessary—she felt that she could do so and enjoy the work. But suddenly the great ship and its surroundings of brilliant sunshine and white-capped waves faded away. The voices of the passengers chatting on deck became inaudible. A great wave of blackness, silence, and despair settled over her soul, and an unreasoning terror, none the less acute because unreasoning, gripped her. Not one human being who knew her knew that she was alive. She had no right on earth. Her place was with the dead. Horrible pictures printed themselves on her brain, morbid messages seemed entering her ears. She turned with swift despair to the woman who sat, half dozing, in the steamer-chair next to her own. She was a pleasant neighbor, this woman, with white hair and kind eyes. Victoria Delsaro, the haughty and dignified woman of the past merged wholly into the terrified woman of the present, caught her fiercely by the arm.

"For Heaven's sake," she said, "say something to me! Divert my mind! I'm — I'm — so hideously, so appallingly lonely!"

Eight years later Miss Helen Van Dorn, of New York, made her second trip to Japan. She had gone once before at thirty, and had loved the country. She wondered now, finding herself again among its admirable toy-houses and flowers, why she had waited all these years to come a second time. Her first visit had been with Victoria Delsaro—poor Victoria! Miss Van Dorn had suffered various losses in life, not the least of them that of this friend. Even yet, she did not let her mind dwell on the tragedies of the Winfield fire. But this day thoughts of Victoria persistently obtruded themselves. There were memories of her on every side in this quaint and distant land. That tiny house, wisteria-covered and almost lost in a small forest of roses and camellias, was like the one in which she and Victoria had experienced two months of the joys of Japanese house-keeping, with nine servants and in four rooms. She recalled the tragic comedy of their first bath, the party they gave for little Madame Hekayamagi, the dinner at the home of the first lady of the village—how Victoria had enjoyed it all, and how different she had seemed from the woman of after-years — the Victoria who had turned morbid, suspicious, and hyperanalytic.

Miss Van Dorn was so full of these thoughts that she did not at first see a woman who had come out of the door of the house, and, sheltering her eyes with her hands, was looking down a winding road fringed with low Japanese pines. It was the unusual gesture that attracted Miss Van Dorn's attention. She looked, and then looked again with deeper interest. The woman was white, and evidently a lady. She was well but plainly dressed, and her movements were quick and graceful. There was, even in the three-quarter view she obtained, something strangely familiar in the outlines of the figure and profile. Helen Van Dorn stared, winked a little, stared again, took four strides forward, and caught the woman by both hands.

"Victoria!" she gasped. "Victoria Delsaro!" Her voice trembled and tears gushed from the sharp eyes behind her glasses.

"I've always had, deep down, somewhere, a hope—a blessed little hope—that I would some day find you," she said.

The other woman hesitated, flushed, paled, and then laughed. There was no resisting the tremor in her friend's voice, nor those most unusual tears in her friend's keen eyes.

"Dear Helen," she said, "what an apparition you are—out of that old, almost forgotten life of mine."

"I'm coming in," announced Miss Van Dorn, breathlessly. "I'm coming in to talk to you."

Victoria slipped her arm round her waist in a gesture that recalled the days of their girlhood.

"It's nicer out here," she said. "Later I wish you to come in, for I have something to show you. She blushed a little. "I'm Victoria still," she added, with a smile, "but not Victoria Delsaro."

She swung her friend down on a low bench framed in flowers, and took a place beside her.

"Never mind me," she said, lightly. "I'll tell you all about myself later. Tell me about yourself and New York."

Miss Van Dorn plunged into her recital. News of men and women, music, literature, politics, society gossip, dropped from the end of her clever tongue in a monologic bridging of eight years. Then she faced her friend squarely, with the high courage of her Dutch ancestry.

"You must come back to it all, Victoria," she said, resolutely. "You must drop this farce, so unworthy of you, and return to your own country and your old friends. Your wealth is still yours — for that myth of a cousin of yours has never been found, although every effort has been made to trace him. Come back and claim your own. Come back to life and friends and civilization and luxury and love."

The other woman had been watching her speculatively as she spoke. It was impossible to read what she felt in her serene face, but under this cool composure a conflict was raging. She drew a long breath. A wave of memory rolled over her, drenching her in the atmosphere of the past. Civilization, luxury, beauty, wealth, and all that these things implied, seemed to call to her across the sea from her native land. The heavy odor of the tropical flowers around nauseated her, and she turned with a quick distaste from the grotesque, familiar little figures that bobbed an evening salutation to her as they passed. They seemed not men, but dolls, and their country in that instant of revolt seemed a dolls' land, fit only for toy men and women. Through the open windows of the next house came the soft twang of the samisen, like a fitting undertone of her own sudden nostalgia.

Then, suddenly, far down the road that fronted them, she saw coming towards her a man. It was a white man — an Englishman, apparently, strong, resolute, good-looking, and with a slight stoop to his broad shoulders. Miss Van Dorn saw him at the same moment, and a sudden intuition made her look with close interest. He was, she noticed, simply dressed, but he radiated the exquisite physical wholesomeness of his race. He was evidently a book-keeper or accountant in some Japanese business house with English interests. As he drew near he caught his wife's eye, and there passed between the two a look of such perfect love and understanding that Miss Van Dorn instinctively dropped her eyes before it. She had seen it only once or twice in all her eventful life, but it was something no human being could mistake.

At the same moment, as if drawn by a magnet, a deliciously roly-poly baby toddled out of the door, adoringly followed by a Japanese nurse. It was a little boy, with his mother's dark eyes and the Englishman's fair curls, and with a marked unsteadiness of gait, for he was just learning to walk. He lurched down the road towards his father with a triumphant crow that carried far in the perfumed silence of the evening.

The woman who had been Victoria Delsaro turned on her old friend a transfigured face. All the triumph of happy wifehood and adoring motherhood was there, together with a sweet humility that seemed strange to one who had known her in the past.

She took Miss Van Dorn's thin shoulders in her strong, brown hands and looked at her affectionately.

"Come, Helen," she said, lightly, "and meet my husband and my son. But mind, no word of my past, for my husband knows nothing of it and he never shall. He may not seem much to you, but he's the man I've travelled this earth over to find, and he has given me the greatest happiness I have ever known. I shall make it my affair to keep that."

She stopped a moment, and then continued slowly:

"For just one instant when you were talking it seemed possible to go back to America with him and my baby, and take up life there with their help. But that was madness. We are happy, we have all we want, we can take care of our boy, and God forbid that I should put him and his father through the bitter school I found there. We love each other, and that is all that really counts in life. This is our home—our paradise. Here we remain."

The One Who Intervened

The One Who Intervened

IT was rumored in the offices of the New York *Evening Trumpet* that Gordon, the city editor, had a "grief."

The exact nature of this heart-soreness was a mystery. Many conjectures concerning it, offered by the members of the staff, were successively declined after the thoughtful consideration the subject merited. The most plausible theories were advanced by two of the men whose opinions usually carried much weight. One of these was by Northrup, the "star reporter," who inclined to the belief that the city editor had a love affair. The other was by Morton, the sporting editor, who asserted that, in his opinion, Gordon's evident gloom was caused by a debt—a large one.

Morton's diagnosis of the case would have been very valuable if he himself had not been haunted by a bill collector, whose patient stand at the front entrance of the *Trumpet* building had constrained the newspaper man to the use of the side door. Recalling this, his associates adjudged him unable to bring to the solution of the office problem the unclouded mind its importance deserved. They therefore received his surmise with a certain coldness. They felt, on the other hand, that Northrup's suggestion was less telling than it would have been if he had not, at the same time, been proudly exhibiting to his friends the photograph of a young person in white.

It was hinted that perhaps Miss Wetmore knew something of the cause of the city editor's carking care. Almost every man on the *Evening Trumpet* had confided his woes to her. Why not Gordon? True, he was not communicative at the best, but man's tendency to talk of his troubles to a sympathetic woman had, of course, some place in him. Every one knew that he admired and respected his leading woman reporter. What more natural than that he should have offered at least a half-confidence, if only in the form of an apology for the curtness and grumpiness he had shown of late to the members of his staff?

If he had, Miss Wetmore had not betrayed his trust. She was conscious of the quiet discussion which went on around her each day after the first edition of the newspaper had gone to press, but she took no part in it except to remark on one occasion that Mr. Gordon's private affairs were of no interest to her, and that such free comment on them in the office was in singularly bad taste. Her associates looked ill-used for half an hour afterwards, but the criticism did not prevent them from watching the city editor closely every time he approached her desk or sent for her to come to his. Nevertheless, they were temporarily off guard during one of these visits on a certain Friday, and with what they would have called the irony of fate it was on this occasion that Gordon for the first time touched upon personal matters to the newspaper woman.

He was looking pale and haggard, and the girl noticed this with a thrill of sympathy. She liked Mr. Gordon. He had been very considerate in his treatment of her, and she remembered her experience with other city editors vividly enough to appreciate his almost invariable courtesy. Something of her feeling was in her eyes as she glanced down at the tired-faced young man who was bunched forward over his desk with depression in every line of his relaxed figure. Perhaps it was this sympathetic expression which wrung from Gordon the unexpected speech that left his lips.

"I'm in great trouble, Miss Wetmore," he broke out, so suddenly that the reporter started. The remark was too unlike his usual cool reticence for her not to look at him in surprise, and then cast an apprehensive glance around. There was a temporary lull over the city room. The first edition of the *Evening Trumpet* was on the presses, and the young men of the staff had turned from copy writing and reading to spirited discussion of the points of a certain pup. The pup was present with his owner, a vividly attired Bowery youth, who bore a striking resemblance to his pet in face and figure. The city editor's eyes followed the direction of the woman's, and rested with quick appreciation on the interested group.

"They're all right," he said, "and we can talk. I have no right to bore you with my affairs," he went on, apologetically. "I wouldn't do it if it were not that I believe you can help me—and I'm afraid nobody else can."

"Then please tell me all about it," she replied, with quiet earnestness. "It will be a pleasure to me," she added, "to do anything I can. I hope you feel that."

"If I did not, I should not come to you," he told her. He leaned back in his chair, closely studying her expression as he went on.

"I'm going to tell you the whole story.

It won't take long, and the boys will think I'm giving you an assignment. You might make it look like that by taking a few notes. Here's the situation. There's a woman in it, of course. I've been devoted to her for three years. Her people object to me. I can't tell you why—it's too long a story, and that doesn't matter. Lately they have boycotted me, so to speak. I haven't been allowed to enter their house. She and I have managed to meet once or twice at the home of a common friend, and to get a few letters to each other, but they discovered that. The result of it all is that they're sending her to Europe. They have engaged her passage on the *Champagne,* and she sails to-morrow morning, nobly guarded by the entire family. They've surrounded her with a human wall of big brothers, maiden aunts, and all that. I've attacked it from various points and it's surprisingly strong. I can't reach her; I can't even get a letter to her. Of course, if they take her off before I can communicate with her it will end everything. She'll think I'm indifferent, or they'll tell her some yarn—Heaven knows what. They intend to keep her abroad two years. No doubt they'll spend that time poisoning her mind against me," ended Gordon, pausing to reflect bitterly upon this gloomy prospect.

Miss Wetmore made a few notes on the pad before her. Morton was sauntering past the desk.

"Last night an inspiration came to me," continued the city editor, more slowly. He had drooped forward again and was nervously fingering the papers on his desk. "It's a fine one, but the practical application of it depends on you. I have managed to get a few words to her this morning, asking her to receive 'Miss Smith' to-day. She will understand. What I want you to do is to be 'Miss Smith' for this occasion only. Call on her, send up your name, talk about your plan to get up a series of parlor readings for the Hottentots, or something of that kind, and the moment you're alone with her give her this letter from me." He extracted a bulky envelope from his pocket as he spoke and laid it on her desk. It bore no name or address.

"I—I—really, I don't want to seem to hesitate for a moment—and yet—" stammered the girl, doubtfully. A dozen questions were rising in her mind. It seemed to her that she should have the answer to one or two of them, at least, before considering the matter further. Gordon looked at her, and his eyes fell rather consciously before the glance in hers. Then he raised them again suddenly.

"She is utterly wretched," he urged. "If I can get her away from them she'll be happy for the first time in years. You don't know the conditions and I can't explain them. I'm afraid you wouldn't understand them if I did. Women don't reason as men do about—well, about these things. All that I can say is that I love her devotedly, and I know she cares for me, although she has not yet admitted it in so many words. She is miserable, and my greatest wish is to make her happy."

His voice grew slightly husky as he

spoke. There was no questioning the depth and sincerity of his feeling.

"There is no sense in giving you a half-confidence," he went on. "I tell you frankly that I am asking her to be taken suddenly ill and miss that steamer to-morrow. That will give me a few days more time, in which I may be able to carry out another plan I have in mind. Everything is put before her here," touching the letter on the desk as he spoke. "Where's the woman in you if you don't appreciate the beauty and romance of a confidence like this?" he added, more lightly. She was evidently yielding, and his spirits rose as he observed this. He broke out in one of his unusual but infectious laughs.

"Come now," he said, coaxingly. "You're going to help us!"

Miss Wetmore closed her note-book and put the letter he had given her into her pocket.

"I'll do my best," she said. "Where am I to go, and what is the lady's name?"

He gave the street and number promptly enough, but there was a perceptible hesitancy in his manner as he added: "The name is Gresham. I thank you more than I can say, Miss Wetmore," he went on, hastily, as he saw that she was about to speak. "I rely absolutely on your help and your discretion. I shall always hold myself ready to do anything I can for you in return."

The office-boy came to him with the message that he was wanted in the business office and he rose quickly. "You're going at once, aren't you?" he asked. And as the girl nodded he left the room with a brighter look on his face than he had worn for many weeks.

Miss Wetmore buttoned her coat thoughtfully. She would not have been a true woman had she not felt deeply interested in the visit before her, but there were certain phases of her mission which did not appeal to her so convincingly.

"I wish I knew more about it all," she mused, as she walked towards the elevated station at Park Place. "Probably they're both wretched; but there may be something to say on the other side of the question, too. I ought to hear from one of the maiden aunts. No doubt she'd be eloquent on the subject," added the newspaper woman, smiling at the vision this thought called up. "At all events," she reflected, as she entered the train, "Mr. Gordon has been very kind to me, and he is thoroughly in earnest about this matter. I've promised to help him, and I shall do all I can."

She repeated to herself this resolution as she sent her card to Miss Gresham by the maid who answered the bell. She was ushered into the library, and while she awaited the maid's return she found herself unconsciously studying the books and pictures around her as possible indications of the taste of their owner. A bright fire in the open grate invited her to a leather-covered chair drawn closely up to the blaze. As she sank into its open arms she noticed that the perfume of roses filled the room, and that a vase on the table held great masses of the beautiful flowers. Low bookcases lined the walls, and above them hung a number of excellent watercolors and etchings. On the large library table were scattered magazines and periodicals illustrating the current literature of Europe and America.

A book, with a paper-knife thrust between its uncut leaves, lay open on the rug, as if the reader had dropped it hastily in response to some sudden summons. Miss Wetmore picked it up and glanced at the title. It was a new edition of Herrick's love-songs, and several of the sweetest were marked by a swift pencil stroke. On the fly-leaf, also in pencil, was the name "Alice Gresham." The writing was Herbert Gordon's. Miss Wetmore had seen it too often on assignment slips and curt office messages not to recognize immediately the characteristic sweep of the letters. She smiled as she laid the little volume on the table, for the few pencil-marks had brought the city editor's love affair before her almost as vividly as his own hurried words had done. She remembered that she was in the house of the woman he loved, and that she was there with the avowed purpose of helping them both. Judging by these surroundings, Miss Gresham was a woman of wealth and culture. The city editor had only his good name, his brains, and his salary, the latter a liberal one, but not sufficiently elastic to meet the demands of an establishment like this. Doubtless that was why the stern parent objected. Perhaps, after all, the young people were justified in questioning parental authority. Miss Wetmore had not felt so sure of that when she entered, and her spirits rose as this solution of the problem presented itself to her as feasible. Her reverie was interrupted by the reappearance of the maid who had admitted her.

"Madame asks if it will inconvenience mademoiselle to wait ten or fifteen minutes," she said. "She wishes to see mademoiselle, but several of her friends are with her to say good-bye. She leaves for Europe to-morrow. When they have departed, she will ask mademoiselle to be so good as to come to her up-stairs."

"Please say I will await her convenience —but it is Miss Gresham, not Mrs. Gresham, I wish to see," corrected the newspaper woman.

The maid looked surprised.

"There is but one," she replied, quietly. "My meestrees is Madame Gresham; there is no Mees Gresham in the family. It is madame who has been expecting Mademoiselle Smeeth all day. She told me to see that she was informed the moment Mademoiselle Smeeth came."

The Frenchwoman had spoken slowly and meaningly. Miss Wetmore glanced up and met her eye. The expression in it could have but one significance. The woman evidently knew the reason of her visit. It had been through her, probably, that Gordon's words of warning had penetrated the carefully guarded household. The whole situation unrolled itself before the reporter, and her enlightenment was not pleasant.

"I will wait for Mrs. Gresham," she said, quietly. The maid immediately left the room with a soft "Merci, mademoiselle," and there was a little time before her in which to readjust herself to the situation. She was trying to do this and to call her chaotic thoughts to order when she heard a gurgle of childish laughter, which floated to the library from some upper region of the house. It was followed by a succession of small thumps, like the dragging of an object down the stairs, and by various infantile ejaculations, vague at first, but growing in distinctness. Then there was the rattle of little wheels, the clink of toy harness, and in another moment a small boy about five years old walked composedly into the room, drawing after him a wagon to which two exceedingly spirited wooden horses were attached.

He was dressed in a black velvet suit, with a wide, white lace collar. He wore also an air of the most ingratiating friendliness. His short curls stood on end, as if through lively interest in the occasion, and every tooth in his head shone as he walked towards the caller, with one dimpled hand extended and the other guiding the mettlesome animals behind him.

"How do you do?" he asked, with blithe

hospitality. "Céleste said somebody was here to see mama, so I fought I'd tum down. Mama doesn't know I tum," he added, more slowly, and with a slightly apprehensive glance towards the door.

Miss Wetmore laughed and gave him an appreciative hug, which seemed to surprise as well as reassure him.

"But I'm afraid you ought not to be here," she added, dutifully, "if mama doesn't know."

The infant responded to these advances by getting into her lap with a confiding smile.

"She won't tare," he said, carelessly. "She lets me tum, sometimes. She tells me to 'muse tallers. Shall I 'muse you?" he added, politely. He had rested his head against her shoulder, and as she looked down at him she saw the creases in his fat little neck under the lace collar, and the big dimples in the hand that rested on her lap. His eyes were brown—an unusually vivid brown, strangely like a certain pair of eyes she loved and had not seen for years. An unusual tenderness rose in the heart of the matter-of-fact reporter, whose profession had long since checked any excess of sentiment in her nature. She kissed the boy softly, and rested her cheek against the velvet one so near it.

"You should be out in the park," she said, "looking for the first spring flowers. The dandelions are beginning to come up now, and little boys with sharp eyes are finding them."

He laughed, looking up at her with eyes that sparkled with the delight of this new friendship.

"I do, sometimes," he added. "To-day I touldn't. We are doin' to Europe. We're doin' to-mowwow. Everybody is putting fings in trunks and boxes."

"Why, that will be very nice," his new acquaintance said. "Perhaps you'll find other little boys to play with on the steamer. Have you any brothers and sisters?"

"No," her youthful host replied, slowly. "There's only papa and mama, and me and Uncle Herbert Gordon. Mama's nice, but she cwies all the time, and Uncle Herbert's vewy nice. He's nicer than papa. Uncle Herbert works on a newspaper. He isn't my weally, twuly uncle, but he said I could tall him uncle. I work on his newspaper, too. I wite fings, and he bwings me money in a little wen—wenvelwope."

He stopped for breath after this struggle with the last word, and Miss Wetmore seized the opportunity to turn his infant mind to other topics. These glimpses into the Gresham *ménage*, while exceedingly interesting under the circumstances, were certainly not wholly justified. She fixed admiring eyes on the horses, temporarily forgotten on the floor.

"Those are very nice horses," she commented. "Do they ever run away?"

"Uncle Herbert gived 'em to me," was the prompt response. "He gived me lots of fings—a wocking-horse an' soldiers an' dwums an' a 'team-car that goes when you wind it up. I haven't seen him for a great many days. He doesn't tum here any more. I asked papa why, and he went wight out, and mama cwied," continued this cherubic-faced *enfant terrible,* the words pouring from his innocent lips like the rush of a small Niagara.

Miss Wetmore gasped a little as if the conversational spray had dashed into her face. She was conscious of the hope that Master Gresham did not "'muse" all his mother's callers by a like artless revelation of family affairs. Much to her relief, he changed the subject with childish inconsequence.

"Papa's pwetty dood, too," he went on, patronizingly. "He taked me to the park one day. I cwied 'cos I touldn't do out wif Uncle Herbert. Papa cwied, too. He wiped his eyes wif his hankfish, and 'en we hed a nice time sailing boats."

Miss Wetmore put the boy gently on the floor. She felt a little dizzy with it all, and longed to think. He stood in front of her, surprised but unoffended by his exclusion from her lap, with his hands behind his back, his small legs very wide apart and his big brown eyes fixed on her face.

"I like you," he remarked, with frank

appreciation. "Tan't you do to Europe wif us? Papa said we will begin 'gain in Europe. How do you begin 'gain?"

Miss Wetmore looked at him rather vaguely, but did not speak until in some disappointment he turned away.

"I shouldn't mind beginning again—in some ways," she then said, slowly, watching the rear view of the child's fat legs he was now giving her as he struggled with the little cart which he had upset. Hearing her voice, he desisted and turned a flushed face towards her.

"I've bwoke my wheel," he said, with the calmness of despair in his tone. "If Uncle Herbert was here he'd fix it. He always fixed fings wight off."

Miss Wetmore rose quickly, and took the little cart from the floor. By diligent work on the broken wheel, and by leading the conversation to the joys of out-door and in-door games, she diverted the mind of the infant and restricted his prattle to legitimate topics.

"If you had a wittle bwother you'd be dood to him, wouldn't you?" was the flattering comment won by the return of the wheel with its usefulness unimpaired.

"I have a brother," his new friend told him. "He isn't a very little brother, but I try to be good to him."

"Would you be dood to me always, if I was your wittle bwother?" was the next question.

"Very. We'll play you are, anyhow. You aren't the first young man I've promised to be a sister to," she laughed, pinching the plump cheeks of the face so trustfully upturned to her. The boy was leaning against her knees, his elbows resting on them, and his chin in his little hands. "I'm going to be very good to you, as it is. You'll never understand how good," she added.

She spoke brightly and decidedly. The situation, as now revealed to her, left but one course open. Her cheeks had flushed scarlet as she realized the part Gordon had meant her to play. It was strange—not flattering, she told herself—that he understood her so little after their year of work together in the same office. But he evidently was desperate, and had staked all on one forlorn hope.

"The fostering friend of such a couple is not exactly my rôle in any event," she had mused, as she toiled over the broken wheel. "When the party of the second part is a married woman and the mother of an adorable child like this, I must decline to go further. They can't communicate without my help, and they shall not have that. Consequently they can't communicate at all. By all means let her go to Europe and forget the man. It may be merely a sentimental episode—and she has a wise husband."

She debated mentally as to whether she should wait the coming of Mrs. Gresham. A little natural curiosity prompted a meeting, but the girl's better judgment prevailed.

"Why should I see her?" she asked herself. "I don't think I'd be foolish enough to let her change my decision. Still, one can't tell, and anyhow a meeting would only be unpleasant for us both." She pushed Gordon's thick letter deeper into her pocket. Then a sudden inspiration came to her and she turned again to Mrs. Gresham's son and heir. He was ostentatiously unbuckling the straps in the harness of his mettlesome steeds, but he stopped courteously as she spoke.

"My little brother," she said, smiling, "I am going away now, and I want you to give your mama a message for me. Do you think you can remember it?"

"'Tourse I tan," responded the small brother of her adoption, with cheerful assurance, "I 'member lots of fings."

Recalling the conversation with which he had favored her, Miss Wetmore felt he was justified in this modest tribute to himself. She took his small hands in her own, and looked steadily into his brown eyes as she gave him the message.

"I want you to tell this to your mama, and not to anybody else. Do you understand?"

"'Tourse I do," said the infant diplomat, again. "I mustn't tell papa. Mama tells me lots of fings not to tell papa," he added, with some expansiveness. Miss

Wetmore promptly checked further revelations along these lines, sorry to be obliged to add to the list.

"Tell mama that Miss Smith made a mistake in coming here, and that you showed it to her. Can you remember that?" she asked.

"Miss Smiff made a 'stake tumin' here and I showed it to her," repeated the boy, slowly. "But I didn't," he added, quickly. "I didn't show you any 'stake."

His lower lip quivered treacherously. He evidently felt that something was wrong. The newspaper woman reassured him with a kiss as she rose and struggled into her coat.

"Oh yes, you did!" she laughed. "You tell your mama how you 'mused me, and she'll understand. It's all right, dear little man. You're a very good boy, and both your mama and I have reason to be grateful to you."

She waited for his responsive smile, which dawned brightly as he trundled his little cart out into the hall after her. A light ripple of laughter came down the stairs, accompanied by the rustle of silk skirts. Mrs. Gresham's guests were taking their departure. That lady's son accompanied the newspaper woman to the door, and followed her wistfully with his eyes until she closed it from the outside. It looked very bright and sunshiny down there in the street. Other little boys were playing marbles on the sidewalk, and there was an organ only half a block away. It was not so nice in the house with mama crying and everybody putting things in trunks. The corners of the small boy's mouth went down a little.

Then he remembered that he had something to do — a message to deliver. He might forget it if he waited longer. His face brightened as he recalled it, and the little wheels of the wagon squeaked as he started up-stairs to his mother, repeating it softly to himself.

Her Friend

Her Friend

MISS WINGATE sank comfortably into her steamer-chair and submitted herself, with the ease of one long used to such service, to the ministrations of a deck steward. He deftly tucked her rug around her and folded it in under her feet, adjusted the cushions at exactly the right angle to support her back, and then laid in her lap the package of mail and the book and periodical whose leaves were still uncut.

The New York pier from which the great ocean liner had just swung out was not half an hour behind. Some of the passengers were now hanging over the deck-rail, gazing homesickly at the receding American shore. Others bustled actively about, settling themselves for the morning as Miss Wingate had already done, but even among these she saw suspiciously red eyelids. She had shed no tears over her departure from her native land, and the distinguished friends who had come down to the pier to see her off had also borne the parting with undiminished cheerfulness. She felt they would exist very comfortably during the four months that were to elapse before they saw her again. So would she! There was not one among them, as she was only too well assured, at all vital to her. Humanity interested her impersonally, but for individuals she had found surprisingly little affinity. She glanced carelessly over the letters in her lap, and, as she recognized the handwriting, could forecast the entertainment or support each was likely to afford. Many of them would be entertaining, a few brilliant—but there was not a heart throb in one of those letters. She smiled as the thought crossed her mind, but let herself dwell on what it connoted.

Why should there be a heart throb?

She had done nothing to call for one, that she could remember. Her intercourse with others was cordial, but never close. Many men had pretended to love her, but her money, she feared, might account for that; and women flattered her, for her position was an enviable one and she could do much for her so-called friends. Now she was trying a new experiment. She was going abroad. She knew no one on the ship, and exulted in the fact. She had dropped a part of her name and was travelling very simply, without a maid. For a time she would be a spectator of life as acted on the steamer's stage, with its human freight as the *dramatis personae.* Then, when she reached Europe, she would work among the poor and do what good she could among them.

The chairs on deck had begun to fill, for the morning was passing. She looked more closely at her nearest neighbors. At her right an open door led to the stairs that descended to the lower deck. There was no chair on that side, as it would have interfered with the people who used the passage-way. The first five of the chairs beyond the door were occupied by a German family of eminent respectability and unmistakable dulness. At her left was a vacant chair, and beyond that several travelling salesmen held forth in animated discussion of the merits of their respective business houses. Miss Wingate surveyed the empty chair with a curious eye. In the place for the owner's name there was a small card, which, without compunction, she leaned forward to read. It bore one word—that rose in black from its white background with almost painful directness. The word was *Smith.*

Miss Wingate closed her eyes wearily and struggled with an unmistakable sense of disappointment, for she had taken a slow ship, and there were eight days of this environment before her. A little bustle made her open them again. The steward, bearing an armful of rugs and cushions, stood beside the empty chair, and a woman was just preparing to seat herself in it. She dropped her lashes and studied the new neighbor

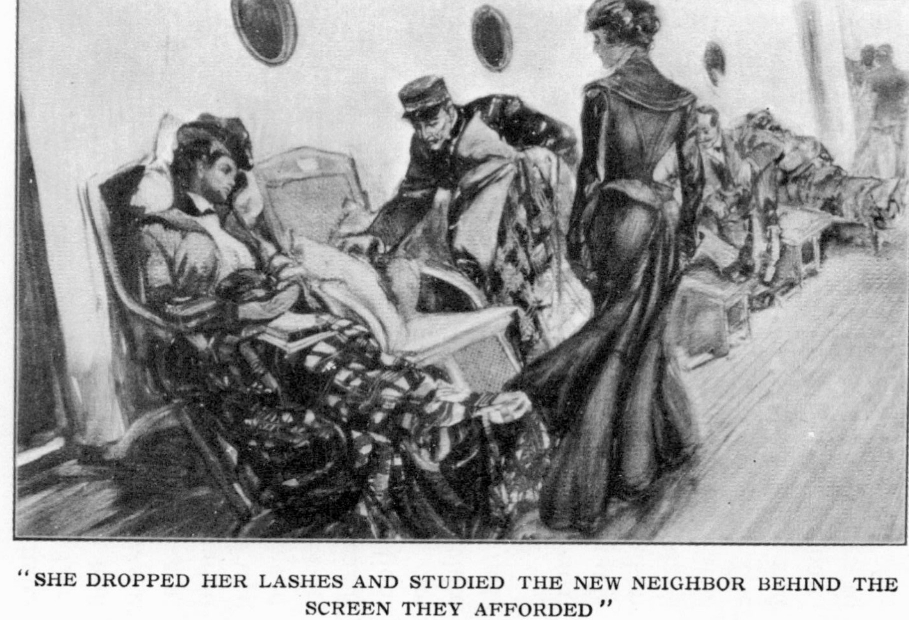

"SHE DROPPED HER LASHES AND STUDIED THE NEW NEIGHBOR BEHIND THE SCREEN THEY AFFORDED"

behind the effective screen they afforded.

She was young, Miss Wingate decided. She herself had reached the age when all women seem young who are under forty. Miss Smith—or was it Mrs. Smith?—was perhaps thirty-five. She stood with her back to the silent spectator, and the latter observed with appreciation the perfection of her figure and her costume. On her head was a small cap with a peak to shade the eyes. Buttoned around her was a tightly fitting reefer of foreign make, with an embroidered collar that came up closely under her chin. Her short skirt was of heavy tweed, and as she settled into her chair Miss Wingate saw that the small feet the steward hastened to cover with her rug were clad in dark tan boots, of perfect fit and style, with rubber heels. All her travelling outfit for comfort spoke of luxury, and the slight gestures of the hand with which she emphasized her wishes were those of a woman accustomed to command and to be obeyed. She did not speak until Miss Wingate made a movement to withdraw her own rug from where it encroached on her neighbor's chair. Then she turned alertly, with a singularly brilliant smile and a courteous word of acknowledgment. The word and one glance of her face supplied Miss Wingate with an instantaneous conviction. "It is neither Mrs. Smith nor Miss Smith," she told herself. "It is not *Smith* at all."

It was true that nothing could be more foreign than her neighbor's face. Her eyes, of which Miss Wingate had caught so brief a glimpse, were very large and dark — of a peculiar velvety brown. Her skin was richly olive, and against this depth of color the whiteness of her teeth was almost startling. Her abundant hair was black and had a natural wave. But it was her mouth to which Miss Wingate's gaze reverted irresistibly. Seen in profile, it showed exquisite curves and a tragic sadness.

Later, Miss Wingate glanced over her passenger list for any additional information it might afford. The ship was a German liner, and there was a long array of Teutonic names, with a liberal sprinkling of others. Among the S's she found repeated the simple legend of the chair—*Mrs. Smith.* There were no initials. She glanced again at her neighbor, and at that moment the first bugle-call for luncheon echoed on deck and Mrs. Smith unrolled herself from her mummy-like wrappings, rose, and strolled below with no eagerness, but a wholesome, normal interest in complying with its summons. The American woman looked after her as she walked down the deck, and the conclusion she had reached earlier in the day strengthened. Miss Wingate had travelled much, and had lived among peoples of varied nationalities. That supple, undulating walk she would have recognized among the women of a hundred races. It was the unmistakable walk of the Slav.

After luncheon she drifted aimlessly towards the front of the ship, and, leaning over the high rail, looked down upon the steerage passengers. They were stretched out upon the deck in various stages of discomfort and cold and illness. Just below her a mother, holding a sick child in her arms, was vainly trying to force some food past its lips. It turned its head away with a wail of protest. She had been conscious when she reached the rail of another silent figure leaning there, and she was not surprised when at her ear a contralto voice with a foreign accent said, quietly:

"We are good sailors, you and I, mademoiselle. Our poor friends below are less happy. How ill they all seem, the unfortunate ones."

Miss Wingate looked into the brown eyes under the little peaked cap and saw that they were wet. The sick baby and the dumb suffering of the others had appealed strongly to Mrs. Smith, who, she knew in that instant, was sympathetic and loved the poor. There was no pose in the attitude. Every line in the woman's face showed that those wet eyes had looked long on human suffering and that she had suffered, too. The idle curiosity of which the American was half ashamed seemed to die at once, and in its place blossomed a sudden sense of intimate sympathy and understanding. She answered simply, as if they had known each other for years.

"They are ill now," she said, "and, of course, they are miserable. But there is another side to it. Most of these people, I think, are emigrants who have succeeded in America. They have saved up a little money and are going home for a visit, or to stay there because they prefer it. The discomfort of the moment is no more to them than it is to any of the sea-sick passengers on board. My heart aches for them when they are coming to America for the first time—when they have left their own land behind and are travelling to a strange country to begin life all over again, handicapped by ignorance and poverty."

The dark face beside her lighted up with one of its irresistible smiles.

"But, pardon, to me it seems that you have it all wrong," she said, quickly. "You are looking at the situation upside down. When they are coming here they are taking a long stride away from misery towards progress. They have left behind them their own land, where there is no hope for such as they. In this big, fine country of yours work and liberty and a future await them. That they had the courage to come shows that in them, in most of them, will be the courage to conquer. America lifts them up. Europe grinds them down. Some of these people below us are going back to that. Already I have talked to them. The mother with the sick child found no one to meet her. Those three men in the corner are returning because they have not succeeded. The two near them, the old men, had not the money to land. So they are facing their grim misery—those brothers of ours whom not even America could help."

She stopped suddenly, as if she realized her own vehemence.

"Pardon me," she said; "do not think I am a platform speaker. But I love these people and I have been among them a great deal."

Miss Wingate responded frankly. She had worked among the poor for years, she said, and now she was going abroad to study their condition over there. She could accomplish more at home, she added, if she knew better what their life had been before they came here. It was not her habit to discuss this interest of hers, but she found herself doing it now in detail, and was surprised by her own unusual expansiveness.

The foreigner turned a sudden glance upon her. It was not long, but in that instant Miss Wingate felt that she was weighed and judgment passed. The idea amused her a little. She herself had a habit of holding the scales in her world; she had long been a just but exacting judge of the men and women around her. Mrs. Smith spoke soberly.

"I would like to talk with you more about it all," she said—"your work and your plans. I can perhaps help you. I know well the condition of the people in France, Italy, Germany—" She stopped and looked out to sea. Far off, against the horizon-line, a whale was spouting. They watched him idly until he disappeared, and then drifted back to their steamer chairs and settled there cosily together, quite as if their association was not to be lightly disturbed.

That night at ten o'clock Miss Wingate sat on deck wondering what had become of her new acquaintance. It was cold, and over the water hung a gray mist, through which the moonlight forced its humid way. Madame, as she called her in her thoughts, had not been at dinner. For an instant Miss Wingate wondered if she were ill, and at once rejected the idea as unworthy. Illness or other weakness seemed remote from that striking personality; but as the thought crossed her mind she modified it, for the woman herself stepped out on deck through the open door beside her, and Miss Wingate saw that she was very pale.

"The child has just died," Mrs. Smith said, taking the other's interest and comprehension for granted, as a matter of course. "The poor mother! She did not realize how ill it was. They never do. And now, poor soul—"

"Have you been in the steerage the whole evening?" Miss Wingate asked.

"Oh yes, since five o'clock. They had the baby in the hospital and the mother was almost insane. Fortunately, I speak her language and I could explain matters to her. But I came now for you to help us, if you will. They bury the little one at midnight—when people are asleep and the ship is quiet. The mother is to be present—they are willing; and if you are there with us it may comfort her. She knows no one, you see, and it is all very terrible for her—"

Mrs. Smith's voice trembled slightly. Calm as she was, she showed the strain she had been under. She looked very tired and almost old. Miss Wingate rose at once, lending herself to the situation in hand with characteristic energy.

"We will do all we can for her," she said, "but this moment it is you who need attention. You are worn out, and you have had no dinner." She called a passing steward, and gave him a few brief instructions. "Bring it here," she added. She wrapped the rugs around the other woman as she spoke, and pressed her gently back among the pillows.

"You should have let me know," she said, reproachfully. "I might have helped instead of dreaming here."

Mrs. Smith succumbed with a little sigh of relaxation.

"I thought it might last all night," she explained. "I meant to call on you later, as I have done, you see. Now we are both free for the time; she sleeps, and one of the steerage women watches her. She has had a dose of chloral, but I have promised to wake her at twelve, that she may look her last on the little one."

She drank the bouillon when it came, and ate a sandwich. "And now," she said, suddenly, "let me doze for a little time. I have not slept for a week, and I have been under a great strain. I feel to-night as if there were a pall over the whole world."

Miss Wingate leaned back comfortably

in her chair and gave herself up to thought. Soon she knew, by the regular breathing of the other, that the tired woman was asleep. Drawing her watch stealthily from her belt, she saw that it was eleven o'clock. Madame had a full hour in which to rest after the strain of the day and before the greater strain of the midnight hour to come. She kept watch faithfully by her side, and, for once in her life, forgot to analyze the feeling that made this service possible and pleasant.

She never forgot that midnight burial, brief as it was. The steamer hung silent on the water for a few tragedy-filled moments, and the faces of the officers and the three women looked ghastly in the moonlit mist. The waves seemed to take their tiny burden reverently, but Miss Wingate felt soul-sick at these rapid revelations of the tragedies of life. It was almost dawn when the two women left the mother, and in the interval they had walked the steerage deck with her hour after hour. Towards morning chloral again worked its insidious benefit, and they were free. They parted at the door of Miss Wingate's stateroom with a clasp of hands. As she undressed drowsily in the gray light of the dawn stealing through the port-hole window, she thought how singularly full and unique had been this first day and night of the voyage. She seemed to see again, as she lay in her berth, the little body consigned to the waves, and the ghastly face of its mother. But clearest of all was her sense of the dominant personality of all those hours, the beautiful-faced stranger who had, without knowing it, knocked at the door of her heart and entered. After all these years she had found a friend. It was with this thought that Miss Wingate fell asleep.

Two women can become very well acquainted in eight days on shipboard, if each is travelling alone and has, for the moment, no other dominant interest. These two hardly realized how much they were seeing of each other as the days passed. They visited their steerage friends, and it became the natural thing that they should walk and talk and spend the days and the long evenings together. In their conversations they touched on a surprising range of subjects. Neither wished to speak of herself, and a week had passed before each realized that it was the exquisite tact and good breeding of the other, as well as her own preference, that kept the topics so impersonal. It was extraordinary, Miss Wingate reflected, that it should be so. They were now at the point of parting; she herself was to leave the steamer at Cherbourg that night, while Mrs. Smith went on to Hamburg. In a very few hours they would have separated, perhaps forever, and neither knew the other's name or home, aught of her family or of her friends. They had met like disembodied spirits on the ocean; they had discussed music and literature and art and travel, and each had felt a surprisingly strong sense of affectionate intimacy—but not a clew to identity had slipped through their lips. At their parting this mystery would leave them as sharply cleft asunder as the great waves cut by the ship's prow.

All these thoughts passed through Miss Wingate's mind as she leaned over the deck-rail, looking at the lights that twinkled on the French coast. Very soon the tender would come out for the passengers who were to disembark for Cherbourg, and in the midst of the commotion and excitement she and her new friend would say good-bye, and that would be the end of the most satisfying friendship of her life. But need it be? Not so far, surely, as she herself was concerned; only too gladly would she tell the other anything she wished to know. But Mrs. Smith's attitude, she realized, was essentially different from her own. The foreigner's was the impenetrable mask of the woman who keeps her counsel for good reason and for all time. In other respects she was intensely feminine and human to the core; but beyond the impenetrable barriers of that reserve Miss Wingate could not encroach for one instant. It had made her own reserve the natural and inevitable course. Under no other conditions could they have reached their common footing.

While they were together this had been of little importance, but now—Miss Wingate was conscious of the shyness of a school-girl as she turned to her silent companion.

"It will soon be good-bye, madame," she said. "Must it be a final one? May I not hope to meet you again some time?"

The Slav hesitated a moment, and in that pause Miss Wingate found her courage.

"We have been very impersonal during this voyage," she went on, hurriedly. "We have exchanged no confidences, and we know nothing of each other. But I have not felt for one moment that we were strangers. It seems to me that I have known and loved you for years. I would gladly have told you at any time the little there is to know about myself if you had seemed to wish it. But I have not desired to force confidence on you or from you; I am not trying to do that now—only"—her voice faltered a little—"I cannot let you slip out of my life without some effort to keep you there. Will you not write to me, and may I not see you some time again?"

She felt her hands taken in a strong, quick grasp. The brown eyes looking into her own were dim. She turned her head away and looked again at the distant lights, for she knew at once what was coming.

"If I could choose to-night a friend from all the world," said the voice that had grown so familiar, "I would say to Fate, 'Let me have this one.' I have never liked any one so much in so short a time. I could trust you — and I want you — but friendship is not for me. I cannot tell you why, though you would understand only too quickly if I could. Do you see that tender coming over the waves? It is coming for you and the other passengers. When you are on it, it will steam away to the French coast, and this ship on which I remain will head towards the North Sea. Each must go its way, and their ways are different. If they kept together, only one could reach its destination. It is so with you and me. It was never meant that we should hold together. Chance—some strange, blessed chance—

has given me these few days with you. During them we felt, if we did not speak it, how close to each other we had grown. I shall remember them and you all my life—and I shall need that memory in the days to come."

Miss Wingate's head sank lower.

"You are in trouble. Is there—anything I can do?"

"Nothing! Or, yes, there is," her friend answered, with sudden energy. "Put me out of your dear heart as soon as you can! But first say a prayer for me, and if, in the future, you should hear something of me that hurts you—do not judge. What can you know of what my people suffer?" She uttered the last words almost to herself, and then checked herself abruptly.

"We are growing very sentimental for mature women with a purpose in life, are we not?" she added, in a lighter tone. "But see, your tender is here, and the passengers are getting ready to leave the ship. Good-bye—God bless you."

She kissed her slowly on each cheek, giving the caress its highest eloquence, and Miss Wingate returned it, almost solemnly, like one in a dream. She heard the band begin the swinging march which was the German ship's farewell to its passengers for France. Still as in a dream she descended the gangway and took a seat in a remote corner of the tender. It pulled away from the great ship and she saw the line of water widening between. On the deck far above the passengers hung over the rail, waving their handkerchiefs and calling good-bye to the friends they had made on the voyage. Their voices grew fainter as the distance between the boats increased. Finally only the music of the band came softly across the stretch of water, and at last even that was silent. The sturdy little tender was puffing its way to the coast; far off on the sea the lights of the liner were growing dim and dimmer.

For a moment Miss Wingate felt ingulfed by the most horrible loneliness of her whole life. Something very like a sob shook her. Then she lifted her head and the pride of many generations came to her rescue. In her life there had been singularly little heart interest, and for that reason this new friendship had been a very beautiful and precious thing. But it was over, and she would bear the disappointment—yes, the grief, for it was a grief—with dignity. She reminded herself that she was a woman of the world and not a sentimental school-girl. And having worked out this conclusion to her entire self-respect, Miss Esther Wingate, possessor of millions, dropped her head on her folded arms and cried for quite ten minutes.

She was too strong and self-reliant to remain depressed. For a few days she let herself indulge in rather softening reveries, in which her lost friend figured, and she found herself haunting the places where she knew the other had been, and dreaming in the Louvre and the Luxembourg before the pictures and statues the other woman loved. But very soon she was again looking at life in her own characteristic fashion—a little suspiciously, more wistfully, but always bravely. She found comfort in working among the poor; "Madame" had loved them, and she felt almost as if she were doing something for her in this care of the under ones of humanity. She travelled slowly through Europe, finding work, and interest in the work, and successfully concealing her own identity behind the name she had chosen. It was characteristic of her that, in visiting the cities and the localities to which Mrs. Smith had referred her, she made no effort to discover the identity of that mysterious stranger. Perhaps she could not have succeeded had she tried; but however easy the task might have been, it was as impossible for Miss Wingate to ask a question in the matter as it would have been to read, uninvited, another person's private correspondence. Mrs. Smith wished to remain unknown—that was sufficient.

It was almost four months later, and the date of her return voyage was very near, when she visited a little city, the seat of a reigning duke. Before she had been there two days she was recognized by the wife of a high official of the court, who had met her during a visit to New York. Miss Wingate good-naturedly and even willingly threw off her incognito and reconciled herself to the round of festivities which followed. There had been several occasions when it had been distinctly inconvenient to be merely Miss Wynne, an eccentric American travelling alone. She felt a surprisingly keen zest in the return to a sphere more like her own. And then, suddenly, the gay little town was thrilled by a tragedy such as it had never known before. A debonair young Russian grand-duke, a guest at the court, was murdered at the very door of the palace. The assassin was captured at once, and on the day of his crime news came to the city of three other attempted assassinations, two in St. Petersburg and one in Moscow, the four revealing a nihilistic plot of far-reaching power and malignity. Had all succeeded, the Russian throne might have trembled on its foundations, but only the young grand-duke fell a victim to one of the deepest, most ingenious plots of modern times. Within an hour the great network of the Russian secret-service system was spread all over Europe. The police had, in each case, promptly arrested the would-be assassins; it was the power back of these for which they were reaching out now.

Miss Wingate was intensely thrilled. She had met and liked the grand-duke—a sweet-faced, unspoiled boy; his tragic fate seemed especially terrible in contrast with the good he might later have done in his high place. Her position as the guest of a court official put her in touch with much that was kept from the general public. She saw the drag-net closing in with its victims, and she met the silent and terrible man who came from St. Petersburg and drifted like a shadow round the court and through the little city. His presence brought awe to court circles; none knew why he was there — this supreme power of the secret police, this man whom, of all men, the Czar most trusted. Looking into his cold eyes, Miss Wingate felt her blood congeal.

Late that night, after a day of great but

suppressed excitement, Miss Wingate's host explained many things with care and elaboration to his wife and her guest. They did not understand them even after this attention on his part; they had a confused sense of technical formalities and foreign laws in unprecedented complication, but out of it all they grasped the fact that there was to be a legal hearing of some kind the next morning, after which, with due ceremony and red-tape, the captured nihilists were to be escorted back to St. Petersburg by the authorities there for that purpose. It would be a dramatic occasion, they gathered, and they were privileged to attend, if they wished.

Miss Wingate almost regretted that she had come the next morning, when she found herself conspicuously placed in a circle of court officials and their wives, the former in all the pomp of glittering uniforms. It must look to the miserable wretches arraigned there, she reflected, very much as if the members of her party had gathered for social enjoyment. The officers were paying much attention to the rich American, and the Parisian-garbed women with her, while decorous as the occasion demanded, were obviously enjoying a new experience. Miss Wingate looked at the line of victims of the Russian drag-net. She was far from being the type of woman who feels a sentimental sympathy for criminals; still, she knew these defiant creatures were merely instruments in the hands of others. Why did they not find the instigators of the plot, she wondered, and make them bear the burden of their crime?

For some time the Russian chief of police had been speaking to the officers of her party in French, a language she herself spoke perfectly. She had paid little attention to his words, but suddenly she noticed that they were pouring forth with unusual rapidity. She listened to his closing sentences:

"And we are therefore," he concluded, "in possession of the chief actor in this entire movement. We have, in addition to the prisoners sitting here, the person who originated and carried out the plot, who directed the correspondence, who assigned to these poor dupes the hellish work they were to do. We have finally captured the most subtle, the most dangerous character in all Russia, whose hand has been time and again raised against the Czar, whose influence has extended even to America, whose brain has inspired half the plots of the past fifteen years, and whose cunning has until now eluded us. Her great family and powerful influence, too, deferred the capture, but we have in our grasp to-day, and in this very room, that arch fiend, the Princess Sonia Alexandrovna."

He brought out the last words with a snarl of such savage triumph that Miss Wingate turned cold as she listened. His face fascinated her, in its vindictive delight. For a moment she could not turn her eyes away from it, but they finally followed the direction of his. He was looking at a little group pushing its way to the front of the room. There were several men guarding the central figure of the group, but they fell back when the vacant space before the court was reached and Sonia

Alexandrovna stepped forth alone. Miss Wingate's slow glance travelled to her face and there rested—petrified!

She was never quite sure what happened after that. She was dimly conscious of a sullen roar, which grew and swelled, and of a mob surging towards the front of the room, and of police officers beating it back, and of one undaunted figure with its brown eyes looking unwaveringly into space. Miss Wingate had heard that a drowning man recalls all the scenes of his past life as he goes down. Long afterwards she remembered that in those few seconds, so full of horror, she had seen not the Princess Sonia Alexandrovna as she stood at the bar, but Sonia Alexandrovna as she was on shipboard—the nurse of a dying baby, the comforter of a broken-hearted mother, the friend of every unfortunate on the great liner, her own friend, whom she had learned to love. Picture after picture of that ocean trip came before Miss Wingate's eyes, as if some one had thrown them on a screen stretched across the dingy room.

She came back to the present with a

"EACH BENT HIS HEAD, WHILE TEARS STREAMED DOWN HIS CHEEKS"

long shudder. The crowd had been swept back and quiet was being restored. Miss Wingate looked once more at the figure in the foreground. Sonia Alexandrovna was looking at the row of nihilists handcuffed together near her. There were five of them, and as her eyes passed in turn from one to another, each bent his head, while tears streamed down his cheeks. It was a beautiful look she gave them—such a look as she had turned on the dying child and the crushed mother and on Esther Wingate herself when she had put away her offered friendship. As if some spring had been touched in her own nature, Esther's tears welled forth, and as they fell the prisoner turned suddenly and recognized her. Their eyes met and clung together. Miss Wingate saw the other through a heavy mist, but, to her excited senses, the brown eyes shining from it seemed to repeat the message of that former farewell: "Do not judge; how can you know what my people suffer?"

An officer touched her on the shoulder, and Sonia Alexandrovna turned slowly away. For just one moment she faltered and her knees seemed to fail her as she walked under the eyes of her friend down the narrow passage formed by the two lines of police. The next she had pulled herself together and moved steadily forward with her characteristic, superb carriage, looking neither to the right nor to the left.

And then, as if that sight were not in itself enough to bear, the court-room seemed to fade away, and Esther Wingate saw the woman who had stolen into her heart as no other friend had ever done, making her last long journey on this earth; walking on and on and on, under snow and bitter sleet, over bare, frozen earth, with captors who wrenched her to her feet when she stumbled and fell; but borne forward through it all by indomitable love for her people to the dumb, living death of Siberia.

Miss Underhill's Lesson

Miss Underhill's Lesson

THE city editor of the New York *Searchlight* was in an exceedingly bad humor. This condition, neither new nor startling, was unpleasant and had an immediate effect upon the members of his staff. Even Hawkins, the star reporter, who was believed to fear no man, after a glance at his chief's clouded brow subdued the merry whistle with which he had entered the city room. The other men wrote busily, or ostentatiously clipped from newspapers extracts supposed to bear on their assignments. One or two, who had finished their "stories," wrote their initials many times on their copy paper, ending the capitals with elaborate and painstaking flourishes. The office-boys remained at a respectful distance from the desk, but kept their eyes and ears wide open, that no signal or order of the editorial autocrat might escape them.

Only one person in the room remained apparently oblivious of the displeasure of the nervous young man who was now striding up and down between the rows of desks, his hands deep-thrust in his pockets, and his teeth viciously chewing a corner of his mustache. Miss Katharine Underhill continued with much serenity the ungrateful task of clearing out her desk—a duty which usually presented itself at the busiest and most inopportune times, and gave her no mental rest until she had accomplished it. The performance was not novel—she had gone through it several times a year for three years—but it never lost interest and charm for her fellow-reporters. Usually they gathered round her, watching the stationery, notes, and manuscript pile up before her, or rescuing with some excitement forgotten articles of their own which they had lent to her in the remote past. They also found a mild satisfaction in reminding her that the dust-covered photograph of a sweet-faced old lady in gray was the one for which the obituary department had been calling for weeks, while the small water-color beside it, borrowed from a distinguished artist months ago for reproduction, had been loaned on her fervid promise to return it the next day.

These episodes, mortifying to a sensitive nature, did not disturb the poise of Miss Underhill. She frequently remarked that great minds should not be burdened by details, and that the exhaustive work of bringing in a "big beat" every day or two banished trivialities from her thoughts. She had further intimated that really loyal fellow-workers, such as hers pretended to be, would themselves have attended to the small matter of returning these things for her, finding their compensation in the credit she was constantly reflecting upon the staff.

The men grinned cheerfully, but failed to act on the suggestion, and so the dust and borrowed articles and photographs continued to accumulate, while Miss Underhill gained the reputation of a "corking good reporter," but one who lacked some of those finer qualities which so ennoble the nature of woman.

Even the most loyal of her many friends admitted that she was careless, sometimes seemingly unscrupulous, and often so sarcastic as to prove that her sense of humor was a trifle too developed. Brandon, the city editor, never gave her assignments demanding the writing of "teary tales," as Hawkins called them. "Teary tales" were news stories full of sadness. Henshaw, who wrote the greater number of those published in *The Searchlight,* was fond of reading poignant extracts from them to any one who would listen, and it was a prime diversion of the staff to have Henshaw favor Miss Underhill with an especially "teary" bit, and hear her "puncture the pathos" with an audaciously pertinent but unfeeling remark.

To-day, owing to the tense atmosphere of the office, she was uninterrupted at the task of setting her desk in order and was making commendable headway in it when the city editor stopped abruptly at her side. In the last moment of his restless wandering around the room his expression had changed from the irritated look of a worried man to the alert masterfulness of the editor who has thought out his problem and sees the way clear before him.

"I have something for you to do," he said, briefly. "Come to my desk and I'll tell you about it."

Miss Underhill rose with a sigh and followed him. She was not in an industrious mood, and she knew by the city editor's expression that it was no light task he had for her. His first words deepened this conviction.

"I don't know whether you keep the run of politics," he said, "and it isn't necessary that you should; but if you can help us to pull off this thing I have in mind it will be the biggest local story we've had in years. It will knock the town off its feet. I've got as far as I can, unless you can help me out. There's a woman in the case—of course."

Miss Underhill listened without enthusiasm, slightly annoyed by the editor's cool assumption of her political ignorance.

"You know, I suppose," he continued, ironically, "that we are in the midst of a city campaign, with three tickets in the field. There is the Republican ticket, headed by Van Nest; the Democratic ticket, headed by Knowles; and the Citizens' ticket, made for the virtuous who are yelling for reform. They have the only good man of the lot—James Kendrick, the philanthropist, and it looks now as if he would be elected. *The Searchlight* is working for him. His prospects are good enough to frighten the Democratic and Republican leaders badly, and they're up to some trick to beat him. The bosses of the two parties are hobnobbing at a great rate and they are probably going to combine in a deal to defeat Kendrick. That is," the city editor continued, patiently keeping his discourse down to the level of a woman's intelligence, "each of the two parties would rather see the other win than have Kendrick get in with his reform ideas; so they are said to have joined forces against him. Then, whichever party gets into power will divide the plums with the other. I suppose this is clear?"

"Yes; but where does the woman come in?" asked Miss Underhill, tersely.

"Right here. We've known for some time that the two big Democratic and Republican bosses have been fixing up some scheme, but we haven't been able to prove it. A few days ago a fool clerk in the office of Briggs, the Republican leader, boasted to his chums that he knew all the inside facts of the case, and had himself hired a room at the Franklin Hotel, where the bosses meet at night and do their talking. One of the chums promptly gave me the tip and we got after the fool clerk. Of course he denied the whole business. At first he even disclaimed having said anything at all. Then, when confronted with the men he had said it to, he tried to squirm out with the bluff that he had just been bragging — telling tall stories to make the fellows think he was a big man. And there he stands; we can't shake him. But he has a wife. She is the woman in the case."

The city editor stopped. Miss Underhill, who had been marvelling over this long recital on the part of an individual usually so taciturn, looked up quickly. "Did she betray him?" she asked.

"No, but she will," asserted the young man, dryly, "without knowing she is doing it. They are an ignorant pair. She was a working-woman of some sort—a box-maker, I think, at Brynsville. His salary is about fifteen dollars a week, and they're both afraid he'll be discharged and lose it. Of course, she must know the truth, and if we get her here we may be able to pull it out of her; and, if we can't, I have something else up my sleeve. Here is where you come in. Get her here on any pretext. It's two now. I want you to have her at the Franklin Hotel at six this evening. I'll meet you there with Briscoe and White, and we'll make her tell all she knows. Her husband doesn't get home till seven, so you won't have him to contend with. We won't detain her more than an hour, and we'll see that she gets back safely by nine. Think you can do it? You can if any one can," the city editor added, with tact.

Miss Underhill modestly agreed that she could. She was interested in the case by this time, and realized her good fortune in being connected with a "story" of which she clearly saw the journalistic possibilities. She planned her campaign as she got on the suburban train and travelled towards Brynsville.

"I'll have to convince her that her husband is in serious trouble, and that by appearing before the committee she may be able to help him out of it," she reflected, dispassionately. "I'll bring her there, somehow, and, if I do, and we get the story, they'll give me the vacation I've been asking for. I simply cannot work another month without a rest."

It was not hard to find the house in Brynsville where the "fool clerk" lived. It was a poor little house with pathetic efforts at decoration, shown by a "transparency" in the window, and muslin curtains tied with ribbons which the sun had faded. The "fool clerk's" wife came to the door herself. Miss Underhill knew it was she as soon as she saw the pretty, worried little face and the worn shirt-waist and tie that were none too clean. The woman's eyes looked as if she had been crying, and the anxious expression in them deepened as Miss Underhill asked for a few moments' conversation with her. "I have something to say to you concerning your husband," she said.

She followed the hostess into the small parlor. On the centre-table lay the inevitable album, and an ornate clock stood in lonely splendor on the mantel-tree. From the floor above came the fretful crying of a child.

Miss Underhill came to the point with business-like directness. "Your husband, Mrs. Williams, is in serious trouble, as you know," she began. "He is getting into it deeper by telling a lot of contradictory stories. Circumstances make the matter very important, and an investigation is in progress. To-day, at six o'clock, a committee of men are to meet at the Franklin Hotel to look into it. You must be there, and they have sent me to bring you. They will not keep you long, and I'll see myself that you are safely home by nine o'clock."

The wife of the "fool clerk" twisted her fingers nervously in her lap. Slow tears gathered in her eyes; but with a certain dignity which surprised the reporter, she kept them from falling. "I can't go," she said, weakly. "They wanted me before, and Jim told me not to pay no attention to 'em. He said I was to keep out of this or I'd make it worse."

Miss Underhill smiled reassuringly. "You couldn't make it any worse than it is," she said. "Mr. Williams has done everything possible in that line. Come now, Mrs. Williams," she urged, "you must admit that your husband has made a bad mess of this. Under the circumstances, his advice is not worth much. On the other hand, you may perhaps clear everything by a few words. The committee won't hurt you; they will merely ask you some questions. You don't have to answer them, if you don't think it will help matters."

The other woman hung back. "Jim said I oughtn't to go," she repeated, doggedly, "an', anyhow, I don't know nothin' about it. I can't tell 'em nothin'."

"Well, then, tell them that," retorted the reporter, good-naturedly. "Tell them anything you please, but you must tell them yourself. They won't be contented until they see you, and you might as well come and have it over with. You may be doing your husband a great injury by refusing this little thing."

Mrs. Williams weakened. "I dunno," she said, doubtfully. "I can't do no harm, I s'pose, an' if I go, mebby they'll leave me alone. But I wish I could send a tellygraf to Jim first."

Miss Underhill rose, promptly taking advantage of the concession. "You come right along with me," she said, cheerfully. "Never mind about the telegram. You'll be home soon after Mr. Williams and you can tell him all about it then."

Mrs. Williams clung to her chair. "I s'pose mother could take care of the baby," she hazarded, looking questioningly at this positive young woman who seemed to decide everything so quickly.

"Of course she can," agreed the reporter; "she'll love to. You know she's never so happy as when she's with the baby," she added, recklessly. "Get your hat and coat and I'll help you with them. We must catch that 5.10 train."

The "fool clerk's" wife still demurred. She thought she ought to dress. She felt she should write a note to Jim. She would like to put the baby to sleep first. Perhaps she ought to "eat a bite" if she was to be back late.

Miss Underhill swept her objections away with a whirlwind of cheery comment. She pointed out the uselessness of a fresh shirt-waist under a jacket, promised a good dinner in town, and laughingly chided the selfishness that would deny a loving grandma the pleasure of putting baby to sleep. Then she hustled the little woman into her coat and got her on board the train in the nick of time. It had all been surprisingly easy, and she was comfortably complacent over her success. She chatted cheerfully as the train whirled Mrs. Williams to the inquisition, and learned much about Jim and the baby and other details of domestic life in the Brynsville cottage which did not especially interest her but helped to keep her "subject" from dangerous reflections.

When they reached the Franklin Hotel the "committee" was waiting, and a light flashed into the city editor's eyes as he saw the shabby little figure in Miss Underhill's wake. He was so pleased that he could afford to be considerate. "You and Mrs. Williams haven't dined, I know," he said, "and neither have we. So we can all have dinner together while we are talking."

The small private dining-room to which they were escorted was bright and cosey. Under its influence and that of the food Mrs. Williams's diffidence wore off. She forgot to watch Miss Underhill's table etiquette as a guide to her own, and she answered simply the adroit questions the committee began to ask her. It soon became evident, even to the most suspicious, that she had spoken truthfully when she asserted that she "didn't know nothin'" more about the case than they themselves. Williams had neither boasted to nor confided in his wife, though he had made her life a burden by his irritability and nervousness since the *dénouement*.

"Now, Mrs. Williams, I'll tell you how we can get at the truth of this," said Brandon, leaning forward with his most brilliant smile. He was a handsome young man, and even the faded eyes of the "fool clerk's" wife showed that she thought so as she looked at him. A little color had come into her cheeks. She had smiled once or twice with unexpected girlishness. Her fears of the terrible committee were quite dispelled by this atmosphere of friendliness. She smiled back at Brandon in a confiding fashion that almost caused a twinge of compunction in that young man.

"Here's my idea," he said, lightly. "Mr. Briggs has a private secretary named Van Alen. I understand that you have met him, and that he has been at your house several times." He looked at her for confirmation.

"Yes, he has," she said, slowly. "He always seemed to like Jim, an' he's been good to all of us—the baby, too. He got Jim's pay raised last year, and he was goin' to try to get more for him when Jim went an' got into this trouble—" She stopped and her lips quivered. Brandon smiled at her reassuringly.

"Don't worry about that," he said, "you're coming out of this all right, especially if you can help us to get at the truth of it. Here is what I want you to do. Go yourself to Mr. Van Alen now, and say you want to have a little private talk with him. He boards at the Evans House, only two blocks from here, and the chances are that he will be there at dinner. When you are alone with him, tell him that you've come because you're afraid your husband is about to lose his position.

Say you are sorry that your husband told what he should not have told—be sure to say it just this way. And say that if he gives your husband another chance, Mr. Williams will deserve it, for he has learned a bitter lesson and will never again betray the confidence of his employers. Then, remember every word that Mr. Van Alen says to you, and come back and tell it to us. But of course you must not mention us, or let Mr. Van Alen know that any one suggested your going to him. He will think it perfectly natural that you should intercede for your husband, especially as he has been kind to Mr. Williams."

Miss Underhill looked at the handsome face of the city editor with keen interest. This then was what he had up his sleeve! He would use the little woman as a cat's-paw, and through her win an admission from Van Alen, when he was wholly off his guard, that her husband had enjoyed the confidence of Briggs and had betrayed it. It was a plan very characteristic of Mr. Brandon.

Mrs. Williams protested feebly. "But mebbe Jim didn't do it," she said. "I 'ain't never thought he done it."

"Never mind that," said Brandon, cheerfully. "You put it just the way I say. If you don't admit Jim's guilt, Van Alen won't trust either of you. And if he should ask you if any one sent you, say no. Nobody has sent you, for I've only *asked* you to go. And be sure to remember exactly what he says, and come right here and tell me. You should be back in half an hour—an hour at the latest, even if you have to wait for him. I will stay here till you come."

He watched her go, with a quizzical gleam in his eyes. They had left the dining-room and were in one of the small reception-rooms giving on the avenue. Looking out of the window, Miss Underhill could follow the progress of the thin, shabby figure, that was pushed and jostled by the crowd, until it was out of sight.

"That doesn't seem quite fair, Mr. Brandon," said White. He was walking nervously back and forth, looking unusually grave. Brandon threw up his head.

"Had to," he said, tersely. "Our last card." He drew a small note-book from his pocket and plunged into its pages with no other expression than that of concentration on his smooth face.

It was almost an hour before Mrs. Williams returned, but the committee did not complain of that when they heard her story. Van Alen, as unsuspecting as was hoped, and full of sympathy for the wife of the young fellow he wished to befriend, had dropped several careless remarks that were convincing in their bearing on the case.

Mrs. Williams was a little alarmed when she was asked to write these out and swear to them before a notary who was called in. She looked at Miss Underhill for encouragement, and that young person promptly gave it in a series of easy nods. Then she took her weary charge out to the sylvan home at Brynsville and left her there to make such explanations as she could to "Jim." Jim was hanging over the gate when they arrived, and the explanation had begun before Miss Underhill was out of hearing on her way to the station.

The night was a busy one in the office of *The Searchlight,* but morning brought reward, for Brandon's "big story" filled the first page, and all New York discussed it at the breakfast-table. That shrewd young man's assertion that it would "knock the town off its feet" was wholly realized, and there were lamentations and woe and much bad language in the offices of the bosses.

Miss Underhill had an out-of-town assignment, and was in the office but a few moments—long enough, however, to receive congratulations on her work in connection with the "biggest beat" for years.

When she reached her rooms that night it was after twelve o'clock, and the gas in the halls of the big apartment-house burned low. As she made her way to the door, she stumbled over a figure crouching at the threshold. It stood up, and in the pale reflection of the dimly burning light, she saw the pallid face and shabby figure of Mrs. Williams. Her clothes were still damp, for it had been raining, and her face was swollen and distorted by much weeping. Resigning herself to the situation without a word, Miss Underhill unlocked the door and ushered her in. She drew her to a comfortable chair, placed her in it, and bustled about to light the gas and draw the shades. Then she poured sherry into a glass, put it on a tray with some biscuits, and set the modest refection before the drooping woman seated near the open fire.

"Drink that," she said, with as much cheerfulness as she could muster. "I suppose you came to have it out with me, and you may say just what you please after you get warm and have had something to eat and drink. I'm sorry you had to wait so long. I have been out of town all day."

Mrs. Williams pushed the tray aside as if the food were poison. "I've been here since four o'clock this afternoon," she said, "and I 'ain't had a mouthful all day. But I'd starve before I eat anything you give me. I ain't quite so far gone as that, yet."

Miss Underhill flushed with vexation. "You can suit yourself, Mrs. Williams, about that," she said. "It isn't much, but it's honestly earned."

The remark was unfortunate. The thin, meek woman of yesterday, who had looked to her for tuition and judgment, was transformed by her wrongs into an arraigning judge not to be ignored.

"Honestly earned!" she flung out. "By honest work like what you done yesterday, I s'pose. Honest work that ruins the lives of hard-working men an' innocent women an' little babies. That's why I'm here—to tell you what I think of such honest work, an' what it's done to me an' mine. I says to myself, 'I may have to wait all night, but she sha'n't sleep till she knows what her trickery done for me this day.' It's cost me my husband an' my home. It may cost me my baby before I git through with it. But I s'pose you've made a few dollars out of it, so what do you care?"

Her anger flickered and went out, drowned by the wave of woe that rolled over her. She began to cry, gaspingly. Miss Underhill felt suddenly sick at heart and at a loss for words.

"Come," she said, at last, "tell me exactly what has happened, and perhaps I can help you. I may not be as bad as you think."

There was bitter rebellion in the eyes that looked over the edge of the grimy handkerchief. "What's happened?" she repeated, bitterly. "There ain't nothin' that hasn't happened, I guess. Soon's I told Jim last night what I done, he got me on the train an' took me right back to the city to see Mr. Van Alen. Jim knowed it would all be in the paper, an' he thought he could keep it out. He wa'n't home, nor nowhere, seems like, an' 'bout one in the mornin' we had to give up an' come home 'cause Jim didn't know what else to do next. First thing this morning he got your paper, and there it was an' made the very worst of. Jim simply acted crazy-like. He—he struck me! He never done that before, an' he ordered me out of the house, an' swore he'd git a divorce. He said mother could stay a day or two to take care of baby. Then he went out; and I never budged. I thought he'd git over the worst of it. But he come back at two and got worse than ever when he seen me. He said he had everything fixed so the paper couldn't have found out nothin' if I hadn't mixed up in it. Then he took me by the shoulders and shoved me out of the house, and said he never wanted to look at me again. I said I'd take the baby, an' he said no court would give a baby to a woman that was sich a fo-fool!"

She ended the last word with a childish wail, but Miss Underhill's sense of humor was obscured. It was unpleasant, this midnight arraignment, and certainly *not* funny. She listened silently.

"An' all I got to say to you is that you done the whole thing," continued the other woman, resuming with new indignation. "You ought to be the one that's punished, not me. You come to me so pleasant an' smilin' that I took a fancy to you right away. It seemed 's if anything you said must be right. I wouldn't 'a' gone with any one else. I trusted you. I thought, 'She's all right; she'll look out for me an' see that I don't do nothin' wrong.' An' when I looked at you that time just before I signed that paper you nodded. I wouldn't 'a' signed it if you hadn't. But I was sure you was lookin' out for me, because you said you would. And what was it? Trickery—nothin' but foolin' me all the way through."

She rose suddenly and stood before an oil portrait that hung over the mantel. It represented a beautiful woman with a little girl four years old leaning against her knee. It was easy to see that they were mother and daughter.

"Is that your mother?" demanded the wife of the "fool clerk."

"Yes."

"An' it's you with her?"

"Yes," said Miss Underhill, humbly.

"Well, if she's alive and you love her, I hope she don't know what kind o' work you're doin'," remarked the woman, almost as if hurling a curse at her deceiver before her mother's portrait.

Miss Underhill shrank as if she had been struck. An idea resolutely kept down in one's mind has staggering force when brutally uttered by a stranger's voice.

A paragraph in one of her mother's recent letters flashed across Miss Underhill's memory with burning appositeness.

"You know my opinion of 'yellow journalism,' darling," the loved hand had written. "I cannot endure the idea of your being identified with a newspaper of that tendency. But I know my dear child too well to feel that she will have any hand in it, or do what she should not do. Still, I tremble for its influence on you, and shall thank God when you secure a position on a higher grade of journal."

Miss Underhill walked abruptly away for a moment, and returned, bringing with her the despised tray, this time containing two glasses and a double supply of biscuits. She set it down before her guest. "Now, Mrs. Williams," she said, quietly, "you must admit that you have said everything you can have to say. You couldn't hurt me more if you talked all night. On the other hand, I will admit that you are justified in every word you have uttered. I have done you a wrong, and I am sorry for it. I will make what amends I can. In the mean time I think we shall both feel better if we eat something while I tell you my plans."

She smiled the sympathetic smile that had won many friends. Mrs. Williams hesitated a moment, then lifted the glass to her lips.

"That's right," said the girl, heartily. She went to her desk and took her check-book out of the pigeon-hole where she kept it. The stubs showed a bank balance of one hundred and ten dollars—not a large sum for a young person whose earnings had averaged fifty dollars a week for the last three years. The mother out West could have explained that, however. Miss Underhill wrote out a check for one hundred dollars, and brought it back to the fire. She handed it to the quieted woman, whose eyes opened wide as she looked at it.

"Here's what you're going to do," said the reporter, blithely. She was again in her element. "You're going to take this money and your mother and the baby and go to the country to-morrow. That will do you all good. Go to the house after Jim is gone—of course, you will stay here to-night — make your arrangements there, and leave before he gets home. I'll take Jim in hand. I know a man who can give him a much better position than he has had, and I'll get it for him on condition that he eats humble pie for his treatment of you. He will be writing in a week for you to come back, but you let him wait a while. We'll discipline him a little. We will make him feel that he has treated you abominably, for he has, and that he is to blame for the whole business, which he is not, really. But that is the only plan by which you can get along with him afterwards."

Mrs. Williams smiled wanly and nodded. The food, the wine, and the swift untangling of all her troubled skein put new life into her. "I guess that's right," she murmured.

"And so it's all settled," said her hostess, gently. "Now you go into my room and sleep. You'll find everything there you need. The bath-room opens from it. Take a good hot bath before you go to bed and you will sleep like a baby. I will forage round and make you some sandwiches. Those biscuits," she added, looking at the empty plate, "are only an apology for food."

When Miss Underhill entered the city room of *The Searchlight* the next morning, Brandon greeted her with self-satisfied cheerfulness.

"'Glory enough for us all,'" he quoted, jovially, "and you're to get a check, too. You're in luck all around, for I've another big story for you."

"Not the same kind, if you please," said Miss Underhill, with deliberation. "Mrs. Williams came to see me last night," she went on, "and told me very candidly what she thought of me. It was not pleasant. It never is, to get a blow at your self-decency. But it made me do some thinking, and I have resolved that in future, when you have such work, you'll have to give it to some one else. I'd rather do even the 'teary tales.'"

She smiled grimly at the expression of utter astonishment on Brandon's face. It appealed to her sense of humor. He gazed at her open-mouthed, without speaking.

"So you, too, thought I hadn't a redeeming point?" she went on more lightly. "Well, I don't blame you. But I have several, and one of them is a suddenly aroused and imperiously active conscience. I shall work along new lines. My space-bills may not be as large, but I am quite sure I shall be better company for myself. And," she added, inwardly, "for my mother."

The Story of a Failure

The Story of a Failure

SHE saw him for the first time at a students' ball in the *Quartier*, and it is very probable that he interested her then as an embodied reflection of her own gloom. She had been in Paris but a few weeks, and was desperately homesick—so much so that this, her first ball, merely deepened the bitterness of existence. Already her New England soul had recoiled from the vulgarity and license which were substitutes for the innocently joyous abandon she had expected. Young men with flushed faces and unpleasantly glittering eyes whizzed unsteadily past her trying to guide the steps of dishevelled partners sadly in need of such help. The big room was close and hot. The shrill voices of women mingled with the piercing wails of the violins, and both beat unpleasantly against her tired ear-drums. She crept into a corner occupied by a couple too absorbed in primitive love-making to notice her, and her eyes looked out wearily over the gaudily dressed figures of the dancers.

This, then, was a foretaste of her environment in Paris. These were the people she had come to live among. In the studio they were not so bad. Some of them were enthusiastic and clever. But they had in them the temperaments which made this kind of thing enjoyable. The young men who worked hardest seemed to throw themselves into the whirl with peculiar zest, and were dancing with the girls who demanded least restraint and whose comments on their escorts and one another were most stimulating. Miss Huested heard several of these remarks, and her sallow cheeks burned. She was very new to Paris.

It was at that moment she caught sight of him. He was lounging against the wall in an opposite corner of the room, looking very much as she felt. A wave of fellow-feeling rolled over her as she observed his depressed expression, his ill-fitting clothes, and his evident isolation. He was so tall that she could see his head above most of the dancers, and get an occasional glimpse of his broad shoulders as the lines parted. She decided that he had a nice face. It was not strikingly handsome, but his complexion was clear and his eyes were large and, she thought, gray. She speculated about him idly for a few moments, until he strolled away and apparently sat down somewhere, for she lost him in the crowd.

She herself remained persistently where she was, declining primly several good-natured invitations to join the dancers. She would leave, she decided, as soon as she could capture the girl acquaintance who had brought her there and get minute directions about the way back to her lodgings. She was straining her eyes in search of this one familiar face when the crowd gathered suddenly at the other end of the room, caught up something, surged back with it, and deposited it at her feet. It was the youth with the nice face. He picked himself up ruefully but good-naturedly as the human wave receded and left him stranded there. She smiled at him irresistibly, and he promptly took a seat by her side in response to that mute invitation.

"I hope you don't mind," he said. "It's merely one of their cunning little ways. They don't like, it seems, to have a fellow stand and look at them, so they gave me this gentle hint." He rubbed his knee and smiled as he spoke. His teeth, Miss Huested noticed, were white and even, and his eyes were brown, not gray.

"You looked as out of place as I felt," she said, cheerfully. "I'm afraid we are both failures as contributors to this gayety."

"I don't care for it," he said, frankly. "And I'm awfully glad," he added, with a little diffidence, "that you don't, either. It's such cheap hilarity, and they'll have such bad heads to-morrow." He laughed.

"However," he went on, "I'm not a theological student, as you may think, and I'm not going to favor you with a sermon at the expense of our 'fellow artists' here. I'd like, though, to stay and talk a few moments, if you don't mind."

Miss Huested's heart warmed to him. He *was* a nice boy, she reflected—thirty-one or two, perhaps, but what was that to her in view of her mature age of thirty-three? She assumed the motherly attitude she felt the occasion demanded, but it soon dropped from her unconsciously as they talked art and artists and Paris. His native State was Iowa, he told her. Hers was Maine—near neighbors to lonely souls in France. They told each other the simple story of their lives with artless candor. His came first, of course. He had been in Paris a little more than a month, and, like herself, had not yet learned French. They laughed together over some of the embarrassing predicaments in which this lack had placed them. He was alone in the world, she learned, with no near relatives. He had worked as a book-keeper in Sioux City until he had saved enough money to make possible the realization of the dream of his life, which was to come to Paris and study Art. They both capitalized the word whenever it occurred in the conversation, and Miss Huested, in addition, spoke it in a hushed voice. His health had not been very good, and desk-work did not benefit it. He thought he had talent, and his friends thought so too, so here he was—this last with his ingenuous boyish smile.

He forgot to mention in what studio he was studying, and she did not ask. She told him, however, she was at the Colarossi; her work so far consisted of simple anatomical studies. Her masters had accused her of draping her figures heavily to hide bad modelling. Yes; she, too, was alone in Paris, and almost alone in the world. Her only relative was an aunt who had sent her abroad, full of touching faith in her abilities. She was very happy in her work. But what did he think of Lemaire as a master? Was it not true that his strong distaste for the merely beautiful was making him the apostle of the grotesque?

They babbled on, the atmosphere of the studios closing in around them. Emily Huested's pale face grew animated, and her light-blue eyes sparkled. She looked very attractive to the lonely young man who had found in her his first friend in France. A sudden sense of intimacy grew up between them; they felt as if they had known each other for years.

He was mentioning to her the faults of the great canvases in the spring Salon when a sudden commotion in front of them checked his words. A red-faced, angry girl, with crisply curled black hair and wearing a cheap yellow evening-gown, was pushing her way towards them through the crowd, unceremoniously sweeping aside with her elbows the dancers who impeded her progress. She stopped before Emily Huested.

"Come along," she said, shortly. "I'm going home."

Miss Huested laughed. It seemed easy to laugh now.

"You don't mean that you've had another quarrel with Ralph?" she asked, teasingly.

"Yes, I have," said the other, "and it's final, too. I'm going; come along."

Miss Huested rose with a little sigh. Edith Clark's quarrels were always "final," and endured with great bitterness until the morning after their occurrence. She felt strangely loath to leave the ball, but she went with apparent willingness, signalling an emphatic negative when the young man's eloquent eyes asked the privilege of escort.

The two girls summoned a cab and rode in silence through the brilliantly lighted streets. Miss Huested was lost in a pleasant reverie. Her companion huddled miserably in her corner, the fierce fire of her wrath already almost quenched by a gentle and refreshing rain of tears.

"Sorry to take you away from your young man," she said, at last. "Where'd you pick him up?"

Miss Clark was from Nevada, and her conversation was not always strictly elegant. But she was pre-eminently good-natured when her anger had not been roused, and she had a happy-go-lucky attitude towards life that won popularity in the *Quartier*. She had singled Emily Huested out for notice because the girl was alone, and her natural kindness made her pity the retiring stranger. Miss Huested did not like her, but she appreciated her good qualities and was grateful for her off-hand friendliness.

"He's an American," she answered. "I don't know his name nor where he studies; but he is from Iowa, and he seems very nice. I'm rather sorry we left so abruptly, for I'd like to know who he is."

"Find out easily enough," snapped Miss Clark, crossly. She, too, was now sorry they had left so abruptly. She buried her dark head in the musty corner of the cab and gave herself up to gloomy reflection until they reached the grimy building on the Quai Voltaire in which each of the girls had a small room.

Notwithstanding Miss Clark's cheery assurance, it was not easy to "find out" the identity of the young American. It should have been, but, though that young woman herself took some pains to get the information—moved, no doubt, by slight compunctions of conscience—Paris seemed to have swallowed at a gulp the shy American youth with the brown eyes.

"I'm sorry," said the Western girl, carelessly, in discussing her failure with her protégée. "He would have suited you to a dot — that man. You two were made for each other—that is, for your kind of companionship, which is to sit on chairs and talk color and technique, and make people feel like shaking you because neither of you would ever dream that there was love in the world."

Miss Clark giggled cheerfully over this conception of the attitude of the happy pair; she had been reconciled with her Ralph in a touching scene, and there was nothing but love in her little world for the time being.

The other woman flushed angrily. She resented the jibe; but deep in her heart lay a regret, stronger than she would have admitted, over the complete disappearance of the young man she had liked so much. She found no one else who interested her, and little by little she withdrew into almost complete isolation, working hard, and left to herself by the students whose sympathies were no longer stirred as her newness and strangeness among them wore off. She toiled indefatigably, but results of her work were long in appearing. The masters ignored her for weeks, then approached her, glanced at her studies, and looked worried. There was something wrong. She had no sense of proportion. Her work was laborious, painstaking — and wholly out of drawing. Students whose frivolity and careless morals she despised were sweeping ahead, making gratifying progress, while she scarcely seemed to have gone on at all.

It was discouraging, but Miss Huested continued to work, cheerfully at first, then bravely, then stolidly, and at the last recklessly. Whatever the mood, the result was always the same — always bad. It was at its worst when the cable came which told her of her aunt's death and of her own penniless condition. The woman who loved her so well had forgotten to provide for her, or had put off the matter from day to day with the optimism of perfect health. The accident that killed her killed hope in the breast of her niece; but she toiled away grimly, for there seemed nothing else to do. It was useless to sail for home. She had no home—in her own land or any other. There was still a little money left of her aunt's last generous instalment, and this she hoarded tenderly, moving into a smaller room high up among the eaves, and eating as little as a healthy normal stomach would consent to accept. Conditions might change—who could tell? She had heard of artists who labored for years to overcome one defect, and triumphed in the end. Why might not she so triumph?

Often, as the days and weeks and months crawled by, she thought wistfully of the man she had met on that never-to-be-forgotten night of the ball. Where was he? Was he successful? If he was conspicuously so, she would, she thought, have heard of him. Was he, too, struggling and being downed in the struggle? She told herself that he was not. There was too much character, too much poise, under his boyishness to make him an unresisting victim of fate. Fate would have a hard fight to overthrow him. She set her lips and resolved once more that it should have an equally severe contest with her. Then she worked harder and ate less, and life cut deep lines of suffering and privation under her eyes and around her mouth.

Miss Clark, like other acquaintances, had drifted away from her and even from the Colarossi, taking a room with another American girl who was a recent arrival. Sometimes, at long intervals, the two met, and on each of these occasions a little twinge of compunction seized the Westerner, the New England woman was so obviously succumbing to the strain on her. Edith Clark threw her a bright smile and a few pleasant words, and later found it unusually difficult to banish from her thoughts the picture of the other's tired face. She decided that she must look her up and see if there was anything a friend could do. Then, soothed by the resolution, she plunged again into her own interests and the matter dropped from her mind.

One day the great Lemaire came to Miss Huested's side, looked gravely at her canvas, hesitated, moistened his lips, and spoke. The words did not come easily, for he liked her: so much that he felt he must tell her the truth.

"Give it up," he said, tersely. "It is useless."

She stared at him with unseeing eyes. All her senses seemed to have concentrated into that of hearing. The voice of outraged Art itself seemed beating implacably against her ear-drums in the master's words.

"Do you mean that there is no hope?" she asked, blankly.

"I think not," he told her. He was speaking in French, and softly, that the others might not hear. "It is, I think, a waste of time to continue; to some the gift comes, to others not. Sometimes there is the love for it, and the longing and ambition, without the gift, and that is very sad. It is so with you. You waste your time at this. At something else, perhaps—"

Miss Huested's world gave way beneath her feet. She felt herself sinking in chaos.

"What shall I do?" she asked, pitifully.

The Frenchman shrugged his shoulders. He had been unusually considerate, for he admired the pluck of this American; but deep in his heart lay the scorn that genius feels for failure. He looked vague.

"There are perhaps occupations in your own country," he murmured, politely. "You Americans are so clever at many things, possibly you have a talent—"

"Carefully concealed about me?" Miss Huested interrupted, with a little, cheerless laugh. She had pulled herself together, and now offered her hand to the artist in one of the quick, frank impulses he admired.

"I shall have to try to learn what and where it is," she added. "If I find it I will let you know, for you have been very kind to me." Her voice softened. "I shall always remember that," she went on. "You have given me every possible chance. You have been patience itself. You have let me stay on, filling a place here which some one else might have had who would do good work. I thank you for it—for everything."

She took off her large apron as she spoke and gathered up her art materials while the Frenchman went to another easel, looking miserable. Miss Huested walked across the threshold of the door, and out into the narrow street. Her eyes rested for a moment on the "Little Tin Chapel" opposite; but she felt no impulse to enter it. She walked on and on, with no definite destination in her mind.

It was May, and Paris was at its gayest and most beautiful. She had been there a year, and she knew and loved each of its changing charms and seasons. To-day the very air was electrical with life and the joy of living. She strolled slowly past Frenchmen sipping their absinthe at tables outside the cafés, past little *ouvrières* pattering cheerfully home from their day's work, past nodding, smiling merchants, barelegged boys, and small girls, who laughed with shrill voices over childish games. At home, she reflected, one sees always in one's walks the tired, overworked men or women whose discontent darkens the fair heaven for others. Here in Paris every one was happy, or seemed so. There was no shadow over this sunshine. Whatever lay underneath, the lips and eyes of these people smiled, and it was easy to believe that all this joy was spontaneous and natural, tossed from one to the other as if life were a game and the beauty of the day a golden ball. She alone, the American, was a discordant element—but she would not be. She drew herself up, and exchanged smiles with the workers and nods with the children. It was her last day here. It should be a pleasant one. She threw back her head and faced her world pluckily.

Her feet turned towards the Louvre and the Luxembourg, and she entered them both, visiting the pictures she loved and standing a long time before her special favorites. One of these was a little drawing in the Luxembourg—a pencil-sketch of the face of a dead woman. Miss Huested had spent hours before it in the past; she sat down now in front of the case that held the precious thing and gazed at it steadily for a long time. All the bitter tragedy of life, all the struggle, all the failure, and all the triumph of death lay revealed in those few pencil-strokes. The woman had lived, suffered, and died—and the experience that came after this was indicated, too, in the rapt, mysterious smile that softened and sweetened the bitter lines cut so deep by Fate. Miss Huested drew a long breath as she looked, and her own expression changed. A certain peaceful serenity, almost triumph, settled over her thin face. She walked out slowly and entered the Luxembourg garden, smiling at the children and the nurses as she passed them, and regarding with a lenient eye the public, unabashed love-making of enamoured couples under the trees. Usually she looked upon these with the fine contempt of a reserved New England soul; but to-day it seemed a fitting accompaniment of the soft spring atmosphere and of nature's fresh unfolding. She felt dimly that she had missed something in life — that some great joy had passed her by; and then, with unconscious sequence, she thought again of the young American, him of the brown eyes and boyish smile, and a little lump came into her throat. The thought of him had become much to her. Was it that, she wondered, which had kept her working and striving so long after her own intelligence had written *failure* against her hopes? She might be frank with herself at last—on this day at least! Was it the longing for his approval? Even now she did not know.

For weeks she had been intensely nervous, her mind full of morbid thoughts, haunting, persistent, hideously suggestive. To-day there was none of these.

She felt the delicious peace and calm of the convalescent whose fight with death is over. All her senses were dulled as by an anæsthetic. The birds in the trees seemed to sing softly, the voices of the children came to her ears as from a great distance, the murmurs and kisses of the couple under the next tree sounded like a hushed love-song. Life's symphony was played for her that day with the soft pedal down. She leaned her head against the back of the chair she was occupying and looked up at the blue sky, letting her mind busy itself with the sweet trifles around her until daylight faded and night began to fall and early lights flashed from the street-lamps. Then she rose and resumed her walk.

Where was he? She wished she knew. If she could meet him now, and tell him the story of the day, and of the months which had led up to it, some things would be different. He could help her—he alone.

She found herself at a quiet spot on the Seine—a spot she had visited the first Sunday she was in Paris, and which had been strangely uppermost in her mind during the past few weeks. It was a silent and deserted place, fringed with neglected grass and weeds, among which the water sucked ominously. A man sat with his back to her some distance away. There was no other human being in sight. His elbows were on his knees and his hands held his chin. Every line of his relaxed figure showed discouragement and fatigue. Miss Huested hardly glanced at him; she gave him no thought after an almost unconscious reflection that he was at a safe distance. A moment later the man heard a soft splash in the river, and looked up indifferently from a distant light on which his eyes were fixed. Then he turned and glanced behind him. The surface of the water was disturbed at one point, but there was nothing in sight except a wharf-rat scurrying to cover. The man listened an instant, heard nothing more, and with a little shiver turned his attention again to the far-off light that seemed to hold his tired gaze.

Two days later the *concierge* of the building in which Miss Huested had her humble room sought the latter's old-time acquaintance, Miss Clark. What she told her spurred that young woman into self-accusation and energetic action. It was unprecedented for the New-Englander to be away from home at night, and an absence of forty-eight hours without explanation was sufficiently startling to set anybody investigating. Miss Clark made hurried inquiries, and was not reassured by the story she heard of her friend's last day at the Colarossi and the interview with Lemaire. The girl's cheeks were white as she went slowly out into the sunshine, accompanied by the faithful Ralph, of whose assistance she had hastened to avail herself.

"We've left the worst for the last," she said, slowly; "but we've got to go there. I don't want to do anything that might hurt her if she is alive; but if she is not where we fear—we shall have to report the case and get help."

They reached the little, low building on the bank of the Seine, and after a momentary hesitation entered. There is a singular absence of red-tape in such a visit in Paris, and no one challenged or questioned them as they stepped from the glory of the May sunshine across the threshold and into the gloom of the Morgue. A large screen confronted them; another step brought them around it and showed them a great glass case, filling one side of the small room. Behind it were two dead bodies—those of a man and a woman. Their eyes fastened on the latter and then turned, horror filled, to each other.

Death, even the death she had chosen, had treated Emily Huested mercifully. She was reclining, fully dressed, against a supporting frame-work, and her hat, stained and draggled, hung above her head. The heavy braids of her hair had been loosened by the water and hung down beside her, dripping grewsomely on the floor. Her garments were soaked and stained with mud, for she had been found but a few hours before; but her face was singularly placid. One of the attendants, attracted perhaps by its delicacy and refinement, had washed it and closed her eyes. She seemed asleep as she lay there, and peacefully asleep, like a tired child.

Miss Clark leaned her head against the glass that separated them and sobbed hysterically. Self-reproach, violent and unreasoning, added its element to the horror of the moment. Her friend crushed his soft hat in his hands and stood beside her, helpless. There was no one else in the room, not even an attendant. The door leading to the street was open, and through it came a long strip of sunshine, the sound of cracking whips, the footsteps of pedestrians, the voices of cabmen, the light laughter of a Frenchwoman passing by.

Miss Clark turned to go, and as she did so her eyes fell for the first time on the other occupant of the case. She stared at him for a long moment. Then she caught the arm of the man beside her in a grip that hurt.

"I've had all I can stand for one day," she said, huskily. Her sobs had ceased and her voice was full of awe. "See," she added; "it is her American, the one she met just once at the ball, the one she liked so much, the one she has always wanted to meet again. And they never met—till now."

She began to cry again.

"It's too horrible to be true," she said. "There's something ghastly in it. It's the kind of thing that doesn't happen except in books and nightmares. Look at them, the two of them, and think of the last time we saw them together—at the ball, with all the lights and the music—"

He tried to calm her. She drew away and gazed steadily into the dead face of the young American with the kind eyes. Those eyes were open, and their expression told that he had met grim horrors face to face. Everything about him revealed suffering and privation. The thin brown hair on his temples had turned gray, and his clothes were worn and patched. He lay with his face towards his companion, and one stiff hand was thrust out as if in greeting at this reunion in the city where both had lost life's great fight.

Miss Clark put her handkerchief back into her pocket and turned resolutely away. The hideous irony of the thing penetrated even her shallow soul.

"They might have helped or saved each other if they had met in time," she said. "I wonder—I wonder. But, anyway, this ending is too much for my nerves."

She turned suddenly to her companion.

"Take me away from here," she said. "Take me out among living things—and give me an absinthe!"

In the Case of Dora Risser

In the Case of Dora Risser

"IF you wish a story of human interest," said Miss Underhill, distinctly, "I think this one would do. It is unique, and has fine possibilities of pathos. It might almost evolve into a 'teary tale.'"

She leaned her elbow on the city editor's desk as she spoke, and regarded that awe-inspiring young man with a serene eye. She was not easily impressed, and she wholly declined to look upon him with the reverential wonder which the other members of his staff affected. It happened, therefore, that the city editor had days of but lukewarm enthusiasm over Miss Underhill's work, and this was one of them.

"Don't see much in it," he said, tersely. "Old woman, old attic, old story. We've done it too often."

Miss Underhill smiled in the slightly superior manner that invariably got on the city editor's nerves.

"Oh, but this is so different," she said. "This old woman — my discovery — has spent twenty-nine years in one tenement-room on Forsyth Street. During those years she has never left that room. She is a cripple, and she sits in a chair by the window, and all day long, with her hands folded in her lap, she looks down on the festering street and thinks. She is absolutely alone. If the neighbors remember to bring her something to eat during the day, she has it. If they forget, she doesn't. Usually, one of the tenement women comes in at night and puts her to bed. Sometimes they forget that, and then she dozes in her big chair until morning. A little Jewish society pays her rent and has paid it for many years, but no one else except the tenement women does anything for her. She has become to them and to their successors during these years a kind of legacy, passed from one to the other. She goes with the rooms and the occupants must look out for her."

The city editor looked bored.

"Can't see it yet," he announced, brusquely. "Can't see more than a few paragraphs at the most."

Miss Underhill passed over the interruption with her usual blithe unconcern.

"What I want to do," she continued, cheerfully, "is to take the old woman for a drive. I want to get her out of that tenement-room—for the first time in twenty-nine years, remember—and show her the world. I want her to see the Park and the trees and the sky, and the river and the boats on it, and the elevated trains and the tall new buildings; and I want to write a story telling what she thinks of New York after her Rip Van Winkle sleep."

The city editor's lips relaxed in an unwilling smile.

"That'll do," he said, briskly. "Go ahead."

Miss Underhill went ahead with characteristic energy. She had, also characteristically, made all her arrangements before she consulted the city editor, in serene assurance that the story would "go," as she put it to herself. She even remembered to mention to the old woman her share in the programme. A small detail like that Miss Underhill sometimes forgot.

"I'm going to take you for a drive," she said, cordially. "I want you to get a breath of fresh air and to have a good time. Then I'll make a story of it."

Old Mrs. Risser looked worried. It was a vast undertaking to her — this drive, and not to be lightly assumed. She listened without enthusiasm to Miss Underhill's rapidly outlined plans of nurses to carry her down the stairs, quiet horses, rubber-tired wheels, and kindred comforts. Neither did the beauties of nature, held up to her imagination, inspire her with interest. Once only her faded old eyes showed a gleam of satisfaction, and this was when Miss Underhill dwelt on the commotion the proposed drive was already creating in the tenement.

"They'll all be at the windows to see you off," she announced, and Mrs. Risser listened with a satisfied quiver of her loose old lips and unconsciously drew herself up in her chair.

The next day Miss Underhill drove down Forsyth Street with a comfortable sense of satisfaction in her breast. She was getting a good story and she was at the same time doing a kindly act—a combination not so frequent as it should be in her reportorial career. She had borrowed the brougham of a wealthy friend for the occasion, and the splendid horses picked their way through the filthy street with a suggestion of outraged daintiness in their knee action. The coachman held his head unusually high. He did not approve of these slum excursions. Miss Underhill smiled serenely at the dirty waifs of humanity drifting behind and running beside the carriage. The odors arising from neglected ash-barrels and decaying refuse offended her nostrils, but did not affect her high spirits. She ran lightly up the three flights of tenement stairs leading to Mrs. Risser's room and tapped gayly on the door. The noise of moans and lamentations from within broke upon her ear, mingled with another more rhythmic sound. She hesitated a moment and walked in.

In her accustomed chair sat Dora Risser, stiff in the unusual freshness of a new gingham waist. Her hands and face offered mute but eloquent testimony to the efforts of a trained nurse who had scoured them enthusiastically and was now energetically at work brushing into smoothness the old woman's gray hair. Big tears fell unchecked on the smooth expanse of gingham over the victim's breast, and great sobs shook her thin figure. At intervals a moan burst from her, mingling dolefully with the cheerful voices of two Salvation Army girls who stood beside her singing a hymn with great vigor. The nurse looked harassed but undaunted. Her eye brightened a little as Miss Underhill entered. "She's ready," she said, tersely.

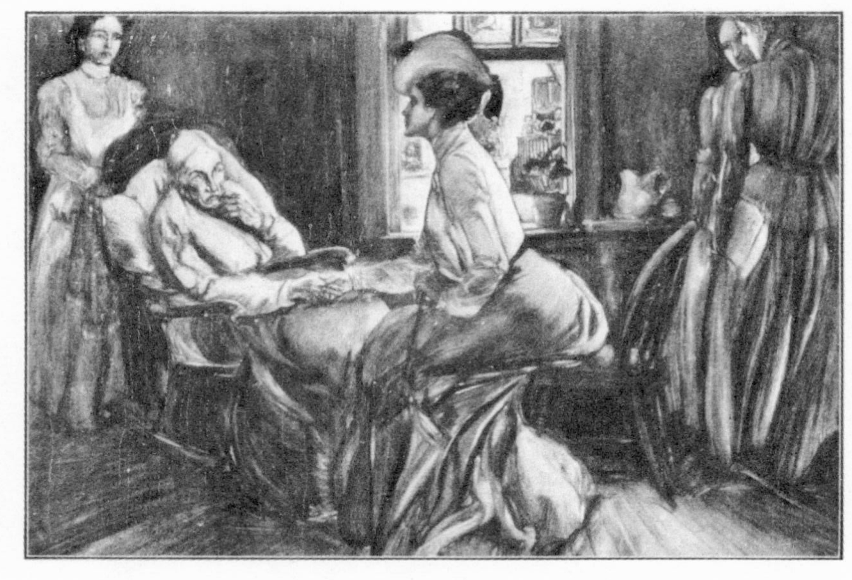

"'NOW, MRS. RISSER,' SHE SAID, 'I WANT YOU TO ENJOY THIS RIDE'"

Perhaps it was the curt professional tone, or possibly a sense of entire helplessness in the hands of others, that made Mrs. Risser break into another anguished wail. The Salvation Army lassies, ignoring both this interruption and that of Miss Underhill's appearance, fell on their knees and offered up a short prayer. Then one of them volunteered a kindly explanation to the reporter, who stood still, reverent but puzzled.

"She thinks you and the nurse are going to take her to some home for old ladies," she said, "where she cannot see the tenement people or have her own home. She wishes to stay here. She likes her home."

Miss Underhill smiled her thanks and crossed to the weeping old woman. Sitting down before her, she took one of her subject's unwilling hands in hers.

"Now, Mrs. Risser," she said, "I want you to enjoy this ride, so I'm going to say a few words to you before we start. I give you my word of honor that this is to be only a drive and that I will bring you back here safely in three hours at the most. You shall return and stay here, and your life will go on as usual. I am glad you like it. I do not intend to interfere in it. But I want to give you one good time. Are you satisfied?"

Mrs. Risser looked doubtful.

"You sure bring me back—sure?" she asked.

"I surely will," the girl answered.

"Tell her so, too," she said, turning to the Salvation lassies. They bent over the old woman and whispered to her quickly for a few moments. Miss Underhill caught the words "kind lady," "nice time," and "fresh air" in occasional staccato tones. Dora Risser wiped her eyes, sniffed drearily, and announced her willingness to go. The men Miss Underhill had engaged to assist the nurse in the difficult work of getting her patient down-stairs entered and the descent began.

The task was a formidable one, but an unexpected factor made it less painful than Miss Underhill had dared to expect. That factor was the simple vanity that blossomed suddenly in Dora Risser's heart. On every landing was an impressed group of tenement women, gazing at the scene with wide-eyed awe; and their interest in the episode of which she was the central figure soothed the old woman to serene unconcern as to her own danger or discomfort. She smiled patronizingly upon her friends and nodded innumerable farewells, which they returned with the stiffness of unwonted ceremony. Miss Underhill's glowing face shone radiantly from the group as she directed and advised in her practical, assertive manner. Once on the street it was a simple matter to lift the woman into the low carriage and settle her comfortably among the soft pillows. As she yielded to their invitation, Miss Underhill was pained to observe the dark cloud returning to her brow.

The horses leaped forward joyfully, spurning the uncongenial soil with their proud hoofs. The early afternoon sun blazed hotly on the baking street and was thrown back in waves of heat from the grimy tenement walls. Ragged and dirty children followed her triumphal progress with shrieks of friendly interest, but all this escaped Dora Risser. She had turned her head and was looking up at the dirty windows of her own little room, and as she looked the tears welled forth again and splashed drearily on the light wrap her new friends had thrown over her old shoulders. Miss Underhill observed them, but wisely said nothing, trusting to the charm of the new impressions and experiences awaiting her companion in the next three hours.

The misery and squalor of the tenements dropped behind them as the carriage rolled into wider, cleaner streets. Miss Underhill drew a long breath as it reached lower Broadway, where the air, though heat-smitten from the asphalt walks, was at least free from disease-breeding odors. She chatted cheerfully to the unresponsive figure at her side, pointing out the tall new buildings, the black line of the elevated road in the distance, and the dark shadow of moving trains; but for these things Dora Risser had no heart.

She cowered in a corner of the carriage, casting furtive, frightened glances out of her tear-dimmed eyes and clutching the side of her seat with a feverish grip. Sometimes she whimpered a little under her breath.

All this, Miss Underhill reflected calmly, was but natural. The great city had grown up around the old woman as she slept, and not even the sound of its heart-throbs found their way through the four thick walls that sheltered her. How could she be other, at first, than nervous and a little frightened? Once out of the business centre, away from the noise and the roar of traffic, and among quiet streets with beautiful homes, she would begin to look about. And when the soft green avenues of the Park unrolled before her, and the gorgeous panorama of the Hudson and the Palisades met her view, the old woman would awaken and rejoice, and on the horrible walls of her beloved room would hang for all time the pictures of memory she brought home from this drive. Miss Underhill, pre-eminently matter-of-fact though she was, felt a lump in her throat as this occurred to her. It was a unique privilege to open such a vista to a starved human soul and mind.

The sharp click of the horses' hoofs as they struck the asphalt paving changed to a soft rhythmic beat as they turned into the Park at the Fifty-ninth Street entrance. A wave of coolness and freshness rolled to meet them as they entered, and, to Miss Underhill's suddenly excited fancy, the great old trees seemed to bend and whisper a welcome to her protégée as the carriage rolled under their spreading branches. The newspaper woman's voice was a little hushed as she pointed out to the old woman the cool, green vistas opening at every side as they passed on. The ripple of water was heard in the distance, mingled with the laughter of little children. Through the trees they got glimpses of the lake and the swan-boats and their happy freight. Tame squirrels sat by the road-side and chattered at them fearlessly. Over the Park brooded the silence and green restfulness of an August afternoon whose intense heat made humanity take its outing lethargically.

Old Dora Risser gulped down a heavy sob and lifted her voice in the first remark of the afternoon.

"I got a geranium," she said, "in my winda." She was looking with a patronizing eye on a bed of that flaunting flower.

Miss Underhill, encouraged by this tentative advance, showed a polite interest.

"Yes," the old woman rambled on. "It's awful pretty. It's got red flowers. Miss Callahan she waters it for me most efery day. I hope it ain't dying now."

She wept afresh at this sad thought, and Miss Underhill hurriedly called her attention to a group of children playing happily on the Carousal.

"We got nice little children in our house," said old Dora, still harping on the joys of home. "Little Josie Eckmeyer iss only four yearss old, but she comess to me efery night to kiss me when she goes to bedt."

Her tears burst forth again, and the occupants of passing carriages looked with curious interest at the artless abandon of her grief. When the newspaper woman spoke it was a little more incisively than she intended.

"You must be very uncomfortable in that place," she said. "How can you bear the noise and the smells and the awful heat of it?"

Her companion looked frightened and ill-used.

"It's a very quiet place, our house," she said, quickly. "We don't never haf such noices like they haf across the street. Of course the womans and the mans has little troubles, but that iss not my business. Mr. Rooney he threw Mrs. Rooney out a winda last week. She was hurt awful. She showed me the black marks on her back, and she had a arm broken. All the mans and womans has their troubles," repeated Mrs. Risser, philosophically.

"But they come in and they talk to me in my little room," she continued, eagerly. "They tell me about all the other neighbors, and they ask me what they must gif the childrens when they are sick, and they bring me little things what they cook. They don't often forget me — not often; they never left me without anything for more than two days. Most always they come in four or five times efery day. Sometimes," here the old woman's voice quivered in reminiscent ecstasy—" sometimes one of the womans brings me a glass of beer."

For some reason she began again at this point to weep with great bitterness. Miss Underhill moved impatiently in her seat. This would be indeed "a teary tale," she reflected, if she put into it half the tears old Dora Risser had already shed. Somehow, this "special" for *The Searchlight* was not developing quite in accordance with her wishes. She turned to the cowering figure at her side.

"Well," she said, briskly, "you're going back to all those joys very soon. But just this moment you are having an experience you will probably never have again. Try to get the benefit of it. Breathe deep and take some fresh air into your lungs. Look about you, and see the grass and the trees and the blue sky overhead. When have you seen the sky before?"

Old Dora drew herself up with a little suggestion of hurt pride in the gesture.

"In my little room, my little room—" she repeated the words, dwelling upon them lovingly—"by the winda where my chair iss. There I can see a big piece of sky, 'most as big as a little carpet. It is blue, and sometimes white clouds go by on it. And sometimes I see black clouds there, and at night I see the stars."

The reporter sat silent, baffled. This old woman, who could find comfort in clouds and stars against a background of sky "almost as big as a little carpet," sat unmoved by her side, looking with eyes that saw not on the new world opened before her. The carriage turned out of the Park and began the journey up Riverside Drive. The coachman let the lines relax in his hands and the horses fell into a slow, gentle trot. Here they were at home. Their nostrils expanded as they sniffed the cool breeze rising from the Hudson. Below lay the river, warm in the sunlight, but rippled by a light wind. On its blue bosom were innumerable craft —yachts, row-boats, and the stately river steamers whose passengers could be seen leaning idly over the deck rails. All this color gleamed against the rich background of the magnificent Palisades looming protectingly behind. Mrs. Risser gazed upon it with a listless eye.

"I got a cat at home, too," she said, suddenly. "She catches mice. She caught one under my bedt yesterday. She catches all wot she wants. We don't haf to give her nothing to eat."

Miss Underhill preserved an eloquent silence. She saw her "story" fading to a dim outline of what it should have been. She thought she saw, too, the cynical smile on the lips of her arch enemy, the city editor. The voice at her side babbled on.

"Sometimes it's real cool in my room," it said. "The buildings iss so high the sun can't get in, and I ain't on that side, anyhow. And Mrs. Eckmeyer she brings me a pitcher of water in the morning, and sometimes I wet a towel and put it on my head. It's cool."

Miss Underhill continued silent. A satisfactory paragraph for the "story" had just occurred to her. She rehearsed it mentally.

"She looked out over the expanse of water, and tears filled her dim old eyes, those eyes which for thirty years had gazed upon nothing but the grimy walls of the opposite tenement and a tiny patch of blue sky which the great building could not quite shut off.

"'When I was a girl,' she said, softly, 'my husband and I used to sit on the river-bank and watch the boats go by. That was long ago—but this makes it seem yesterday.' Her lips quivered a little."

Miss Underhill was conscious of a sudden interruption. The real Dora, not the Dora of her "story," was sobbing again at her side.

"Where are we going?" she whimpered. "We have went so far. Are we in another city? I don't feel well. I think I catch cold. I got some good medicine in my house wot the Salvation girls give me. It always makes me well. It cures anything wot I got."

Miss Underhill addressed the coachman.

"Drive back," she said, curtly. Then she turned to old Dora with her charming smile. She had recovered her good-humor when the reflection occurred to her that her story could tell what Dora Risser *should* have felt during that drive. No one would be the wiser, and Dora herself, once back in her tenement-room, would no doubt corroborate any recital in which she had played a touching and admirable rôle.

"We're going home now," said the reporter, cheerfully. "We will be there in three-quarters of an hour."

Mrs. Risser looked doubtful and her suspicions were intensified by the fact that the coachman returned by a different route, kindly desiring to give the old woman all possible variety. He, too, was more cheerful. The drive was almost over and Miss Underhill's prospective tip pleasantly in the foreground of his thoughts. He suddenly remembered with a twinge of conscience that she was invariably very generous on these occasions. Mrs. Risser seized the side of the carriage with a firmer grip, sat as near the edge of the seat as she dared, looked at the unfamiliar route with scared eyes, and contributed another copious flow of tears to the collection of stains on the borrowed shawl. Beside her the reporter, whose mind was now at rest, mentally outlined telling bits of her "story."

"The carriage turned into the evil-smelling tenement street, from whose refuse-covered cobble-stones the heat seemed to rise in a perceptible haze. Old Dora Risser gave one last long backward look at the world she was leaving—the beautiful world that lay so near to and yet so hideously far from that little tenement-room. Then her gaze rested on the crowded streets, the half-naked children playing in the gutters, the swarming life of the tenement. A change passed

over her face; her features twisted for a moment, but with a mighty effort she forced them into calm. This was her life: she must return to it, for He who put her there had some good purpose in it. She seized the reporter's hand and kissed it.

"'Good-bye,' she said. 'Thank you, and God bless you. You have shown me to-day a glimpse of what I hope awaits me after I take my next—and last—long drive.'"

"That will do pretty well for an ending," reflected Miss Underhill, comfortably, "when I've polished it up a bit. Of course I must make her an educated woman who has seen better days."

A movement beside her aroused her from her pleasant reverie. The carriage had reached the tenement region, and was rolling swiftly through its swarming streets. It was growing late and the push-cart men and peddlers were coming home after their day's work. Some Chinese laundrymen had left their ironing-boards for a breath of air and were sitting on the curb exchanging repartee in pigeon-

English with a little group of hoodlums. A few feet away, a street organ was grinding out an ancient waltz, and several ragged little girls were dancing to the music. A long gasp of delight fell on Miss Underhill's ear. It came from the lips of Dora Risser, who was sitting up gazing around her with shining eyes. She craned her neck to look at the tenements that fell behind them. The carriage turned a corner sharply and entered another street, a shade filthier, more crowded, more evil-smelling than the last. Two drunken men lurched uncertainly along the sidewalk. Dora Risser sent her glance wide-eyed down the street until it lit and rested on a scrubby tenement in one of whose windows bloomed a red geranium. She clutched Miss Underhill's arm with quivering fingers and uttered a shrill cry. Her face was transfigured. The listless, sick little old woman had become an ecstatic creature, hysterical with joy.

"Ach Gott!" she shrieked, *"Ach Gott!*—there's my little home. I'm back again, I'm back." She closed her eyes and

"THE CARRIAGE TURNED A CORNER SHARPLY AND ENTERED ANOTHER STREET"

struggled for breath. "*Ach Gott!*" she gasped. "*Gott sei dank!*"

The nurse and the bearers were waiting, and they carried the happy old woman up the dirty stairs. Her exclamations of delight and her beaming face left no doubt in their minds as to the success of Miss Underhill's experiment. That young lady herself lingered for a confidential last word when the others had departed. She had given the friendly Mrs. Eckmeyer money for the purchase of an evening meal, and the little room was full of the smell of frying meat. Miss Underhill held out her hand, which old Dora Risser did not hasten to kiss. She put her own into it, limply.

"Come now," said the girl, "say you've had a good time."

The old woman hesitated. A shiver passed over her as memory brought up for an instant the terrors of the day. Then her nostrils caught and drew in the mingled odor of frying eggs, bacon, and hot coffee. After all, it was over and she was home. Why bear malice? She grinned good-naturedly.

"Ach, yes," she said, handsomely. "I hat a goot time. Sure!"

It was a very "teary tale" Miss Underhill turned in to the city editor. New York wept over it the following morning. So many letters poured into *The Searchlight* office offering the old woman homes of all degrees of luxury that Miss Underhill was forced to write a brief supplementary article explaining that Dora Risser was "permanently and happily provided for" through *The Searchlight's* efforts.

To the writer of this simple narrative she told the plain, unvarnished facts, and generously added the moral lesson the episode had taught her.

"I think of it," she said, "when I go to all these sociological meetings and hear people worrying about relieving the condition of the poor. I sympathize heartily with that work. But I have learned this lesson very well: that there are times when what the poor want more than they want anything else on earth is simply —to be let alone!"

A Collaboration

A Collaboration

THE Author leaned back comfortably in his easy-chair and looked at the young man. He was a young man himself, but a pre-eminently successful one—so recently successful, too, that the fine flavor of his own greatness was still deliciously fresh on his tongue. He would have been more than human had he remained wholly unspoiled by the popular clamor over his short stories and the remarkable sale of his first novel, now in its three-hundredth edition. As it was, he was very human, hence slightly spoiled, but still young—so young that he had adopted a few mannerisms as fitting accompaniments of acknowledged genius. He narrowed his eyes now, for instance, which he would not have done last year, and looked at his caller through an effective fringe of brown lashes.

"Yes," he said, incisively, "I want a secretary, but I'm afraid I require a little more of one than usual. I need a man who can answer my letters, talk to my publishers, look after my manuscripts, take dictation, if I can ever learn to dictate" — this with modest insinuation of the irksomeness of such restraint — "look up all sorts of things for me, and—er—make himself generally useful. That, of course, I presume you are prepared to do?" he concluded, interrogatively.

The applicant for this responsible post smiled slightly as he quietly replied: "Quite. I'll do my best, and, of course, if I don't suit you can pack me off." He hesitated a moment. "I admire your work tremendously," he added, "and I shall be proud to have even a secretary's small part in it."

The Author smiled back with appreciation. The strong attraction he had felt in this quiet young man at the start was not weakened by his remark.

"Then we'll call it a bargain," he said, cordially. "You've encouraged me to tell you what I consider the most important of your duties. My secretary must listen to my plots! I cannot write a line until I have the whole thing in my head, and I cannot get it properly shaped in my head until I've talked it over with some one I'm sure I'm not boring—or at least," he added, quickly, "somebody whose attention I have a right to expect. As I talk, my ideas shape themselves, my plot develops, my characters begin to get their cues, and—*voilà!* —the story is ready to write."

The eyes of the secretary took on a sudden gleam of interest. They were sombre eyes, and the expression of his striking face was very serious. The brown hair over his temples, too, was powdered with white, and there were lines in his forehead which suggested strong chapters in his duodecimo volume of life.

"I think I can promise to be an attentive auditor," he remarked. "The terms I mentioned in my reply to your note are, I suppose, satisfactory?"

The Author was regarding him in an absent-minded manner.

"Oh yes, yes," he said, hastily. "I am willing to give you what you want if you can do what I want. I wish," he continued, slowly, "that you could begin right away. I've been wasting this morning trying to put a half-digested thing on paper, and if you could stay and let me tell you the facts—"

Mr. Mardenredd, who had risen with the idea that the interview was over, resumed his chair and an attentive manner as the first act of his secretaryship. The Author, charmed by the mute eloquence of this simple act, slapped him boyishly on the shoulder.

"Good!" he said, buoyantly. "Take that big chair near the fire and light a cigar. I'm willing to have my victims made as comfortable as possible. One thing—don't interrupt me when I'm speaking, please, for I may lose a point if you do. But when I stop to think, if any criticism occurs to you, let me have it."

He lit a fresh cigar himself and leaned

back for a few moments collecting his thoughts. Hickory logs burned brilliantly behind the brass andirons, the pure flame pulsing a rich blue or green now and then from the driftwood that had been flung upon them.

"Here's the plot," began the Author, briskly. "It's true, too. I saw some of it work out, and got more of it, piecemeal, from persons who knew the chief actors. My trouble now is to decide whether I'll use it as it is, or touch it up a bit, or perhaps a great deal. Of course I shall change it so that the originals will not be recognized in print. The characters are a Madame Fleury—we'll call her that; her daughter—we'll call her Lily; and a young man—well, he can be *The* Young Man. I shall have to get taking names for them, but I'm going to call the girl Lily anyhow. Madame Fleury was a woman of the town. Some women are born bad, some achieve badness, and some have badness thrust upon them. Madame Fleury distinctly belonged to the third class. But she had it thrust on her just the same, and that is why I put it baldly at first.

"She was a handsome woman, comparatively young, and rather attractive. She owned a big house in a large Western city, and it was furnished with surprisingly good taste. She had books, pictures, tapestries, choice china, plate, and all that sort of thing. She was a fine musician with a good voice. You see, she was a remarkable type. In her native France, in the radiant glow of youth and virtue, she must have been stunning. It makes it very likely that the key to her subsequent career was a Russian grand-duke who figured in the earliest stories of her. Well, her house was a gambling one, where young fellows ruined themselves at cards. You see this story is not exactly *virginibus puerisque.*"

The secretary inclined his head slightly without committing himself to any definite view, and the Author went on:

"Madame Fleury had a daughter, who had spent her girlhood in a convent and knew absolutely nothing of her mother's real character. The woman had been wise enough to select a convent in the extreme East—and the child grew to womanhood there. During the summers her mother took her to small watering-places so remote from the usual haunts there was not one chance in a thousand that any one would recognize her. People never did, or if they did they made no sign, and all went well until the girl was about sixteen, when she suddenly telegraphed that she was coming home, to the city where her mother lived, and which she herself had never been permitted to visit. 'By the time this reaches you,' she wired, 'I shall be in the train.' That meant that she would reach 'home' in two days.

"Madame Fleury was a woman quick to think and act. Nothing could stop Lily now. It therefore behooved her to be ready for this dutiful visit. She went at once to the office of a prominent real-estate man whom she knew and told him of her predicament. He helped her out. He rented to her for one week a fine house, elegantly furnished, in the suburbs of the city, and Madame Fleury spent the next two days getting bric-à-brac, books, pictures, and all that into the place to give it an air of being occupied.

"You can imagine that she had her hands full, but she was equal to the occasion, and when the train from New York steamed into the station Madame Fleury was there to greet her daughter. She took the girl to the house and suddenly succumbed to an attáck of grip, so exhausting in its nature that she could neither go out nor receive guests. Lily, who loved her mother ardently, spent the week in affectionate attendance on her in the sick-room, and at the end of it, as madame's condition urgently required change of climate, the two went off to a remote resort—and that danger was over. The episode shows the length to which she would go for her child.

"One year later Lily was graduated. This meant a mighty problem for Madame Fleury, but she had pondered it well and was ready with her solution when the time came. She turned her house over to a manager and prepared for an absence of two years. Then she went to the Eastern convent and attended the graduation exercises of her daughter — saw her get her diploma. Lily was a beauty by this time—tall and slender, and with the most exquisitely pure face. She must have looked like a lily as she stood in her white gown among the palms and ferns banked on the stage in the great exhibition hall. She was the bright star of the occasion, for she had the valedictory and she sang and played first violin in the orchestra, and did it all wonderfully well; while down among the audience Madame Fleury, in her rich but severe costume of black silk, sat and gazed with her soul in her eyes at this idol of hers—this one thing in her life that was clean. She adored the girl—my story will show that if it shows nothing else; but it must show other things too, and there's the rub."

The Author paused a moment. Perhaps he expected a remark from his auditor, but that young man remained silent, his eyes fixed on the cheery fire. The Author felt that he was thoroughly attentive, however, and, he thought, interested.

"After the graduation exercises," he resumed, "Madame Fleury had a brief interview with the Superior and the nuns with whom her daughter had lived so long, and told them she intended to take her child abroad for two years of travel, and that they were to sail the following Saturday. She regarded with sweet, maternal sympathy Lily's parting with her classmates and the nuns; she saw her folded in the arms of the sisters, and she herself kissed some of Lily's special friends, because her instinct told her the girl would be pleased by that demonstration. She became also almost friendly with their mothers. She was in the convent two days, and in that time seemed, in a way, to wash herself clean. She had flung the past behind her, for a time at least; she was on the edge of a life as new to her as to her daughter, and it was well that before plunging into this unknown phase of things, before stepping from the shadow of a *déclassée* into the sunshine of the respectable, she should have the preparation of those days in the cool silence of the cloister. Her thoughts during that time must have been strange ones. I must work that up in the story."

The Author lit a fresh cigar. He wondered whether it would do to tell the secretary that he didn't mind if he made an occasional comment. But he went on.

"They sailed, and as this is not a chronicle of a *jeune fille's* first pilgrimage abroad, we'll cut that part of it out. They saw things, of course, as they drifted about for the greater part of two years in a quiet and exceedingly conventional fashion. But there was just one object in Europe of which Madame Fleury was in search —and that was the right husband for her daughter. It was he she had come there expressly to find, and every man they met was searched to his very soul by those worldly eyes that had seen so much of life and—men. They met quantities of them, for Lily was charming, and the pair radiated culture, breeding, and wealth. Madame Fleury was playing her supreme rôle on life's stage, and she played it magnificently. I met them during that time, and not until years afterwards did I have an inkling of the truth about them. When a man who was not the right man seemed to interest Lily —and it was easy for 'most any man to interest her, for she was full of romance—the Fleurys suddenly disappeared. It was not done crudely, as you may imagine. Some interesting expedition presented itself, or a remote corner of Europe took on new interest, or a standing invitation was recalled. Lily suspected nothing; instead, she promptly forgot, for she was young, and there were other men in the new foreground. This was the situation when the two, after twenty months of wandering, found themselves in the island of Rugen and, one day, in the presence of a new young man."

The new secretary straightened himself and pulled down his waistcoat. He also crossed his legs. It was something. He evidently recognized the entrance of *The* Young Man.

A Collaboration

"He was a good-enough fellow, I believe," continued the Author, a trifle patronizingly—"excellent family, Oxford, Heidelberg, and all the world after that. He was handsome, too, I'm told, and he swept the girl off her feet. He fell deeply in love with Lily, and the sojourn on the island of Rugen was prolonged. The lovers made their marvellous discoveries of beauties in life hitherto unsuspected, and as they called each other's attention to these things Madame Fleury looked on. *The* Young Man was wise enough to cultivate her as well as her daughter. But it was not necessary. Her motive was too utterly unselfish. She decided that he would do. He was poor, but that was rather a good point. She had turned the searchlight of her investigations on his past, and she found no dark corners. He was all right. He was the man she had scoured Europe to find.

"When *The* Young Man asked Madame Fleury for Lily she had a long talk with him. She told him the whole story, not sparing herself in the least, and at the end she made him a proposition. She asked him to hear it through before he answered it.

"'You may marry my daughter,' she said, 'on one condition—that you and she never return to America. You must make your home here for the remainder of your lives. The day before your marriage I will turn over to her about seventy thousand dollars in stocks and bonds. The day after your marriage I will sail for America. For a few months I will write to my daughter; but within a year she will receive a cable that I am dead—and, so far as she shall ever know, I will be dead from that time forth. But I shall wish to know how it is with her, and at intervals—perhaps two or three times a year—I would like you to write me of her. Do you agree, my friend?'

"*The* Young Man agreed. He was probably touched; he certainly ought to have been by that magnificent, unselfish devotion—by the true mother looming so grandly out of the wreck of the woman. He agreed, and everything was done as

Madame Fleury had arranged. They were married, she sailed for America, and the husband and wife went to Spain on their honeymoon. The parting from her mother was the only suffering the daughter's life had known, but she got over it with the sublime selfishness of youth and love. Her husband was with her—what else mattered? Madame Fleury had, naturally, not quite the same point of view. I can see the chance for good work on what that parting—that final parting—meant to her. She left her daughter to her honeymoon among the jasmine and the nightingales, and she returned to her old life! What else could she do when she had converted everything she possessed into money and given it to her child? She went back, a broken-hearted woman, a poor woman, no longer young, to the life she had learned to loathe—but the lovers in Spain were happy."

The secretary's cigar had gone out. He leaned forward, tossed it into the cheery flames, and accepted another courteously offered by the Author.

"From this point in the tale," resumed the latter, with a slight importance, "Fate advances on my character like the Hellenic Nemesis. Madame Fleury found when she returned to her old haunts that, even in two years, she had been forgotten. Her one friend had died, and others had systematically robbed her right and left. She struggled on, making a brave fight, but life and fate and a broken heart were too much for her. She developed an incurable disease and died by inches, sinking deeper and deeper into poverty, pain, and misery. It took years to bring all this about, but it came slowly and implacably, and she never moaned. She had kept her bargain to the letter. Eleven months after her return to America she had sent the promised cable announcing her death. Lily had cried passionately and drooped for a few weeks, but she got over it, for her husband was still the lover and now her one stay, with her mother dead, as she thought, thousands of miles away. So, when the years had brought poverty and suffering to Madame Fleury, she was helpless and alone; she could not appeal to her only child even had she wished to in her sore need. For *The* Young Man had not kept his part of the bargain as well as she had kept hers.

"After the first two years he never wrote her, and at thc last, added to her physical suffering, she had the mental agony of not knowing whether her daughter, for whom she had sacrificed so much, was ill or well, happy or miserable, alive or dead.

"One old negro servant stayed with her to the end. Long after her death, when it was too late to help, I met this old creature and heard from her the story of those last days — and grim enough it was with its bleak background of tenement, and the dying woman praying to the last that she might know of her child before she went, that she could not leave the world with Lily in it, alone or unhappy. They had not enough to eat —she and the old negress. Then Fate showed its ingenuity by adding a final touch to the tragedy; for one day, when the negress was out for a few moments (begging, she afterwards told me), the pain perhaps was too great for endurance, or possibly there came a moment of insanity. Anyhow, Madame Fleury closed the chapter and thrust herself out of a world on the other side of which, all unsuspecting, lived the child she loved. The last thing she was ever heard to say was very characteristic, a fitting *finale,* I thought, for it was this: She whispered to the old negress during the day, 'I would do it all over again, a hundred times, if I could know for just one instant at the last that she is alive and happy.' And then she added, 'Of one thing, thank God, I am sure. Wherever she is, she is good—my baby, my white flower, my Lily. And if she is that, she cannot be all unhappy. I am content.'"

The Author stopped again and lit a fresh cigar. His face was flushed, and all his little mannerisms had dropped from him, as conventionalities flit in moments of excitement. He was in earnest and deeply interested in his story. His secretary had bent forward in his chair and was staring at the leaping flames with sombre eyes.

"That was the end of Madame Fleury," resumed the Author, more quietly. "And, unfortunately, it is the end of the story as far as my knowledge goes. For I have not the faintest idea what became of the girl. She was never heard of, on this side, after her marriage. I dare say she is leading a peaceful existence in the sunny content of some English home. But I can't present her with four babies, two dogs, and a tea-basket, and end the story that way. It must have a fitting climax, and what that is to be I can't decide. Several things have suggested themselves, but I don't fancy them."

"How would this appeal to you?" said the secretary. He went on slowly, his gaze still bent on the fire:

"You left the lovers in Spain. They have an ideal honeymoon there. But even during those weeks of youth and love and jasmine and nightingale and tinkling mandolin, *The* Young Man begins to remark a strange restlessness in the girl he has married. He does not like it nor understand it, but he tries to think it is the natural exuberance of the convent girl, housed in a cloister all her life and then suddenly brought face to face with a new and fascinating world. He has no doubt that she loves him, and the expressions of her restlessness are harmless enough in the beginning. He loves her enough to watch her pretty closely, and he thinks she will soon get used to her new freedom and independence, and quiet down. So he almost enjoys the energy she shows in looking for excitement.

"Let him adore her, and gratify all her whims, taking her from place to place as her caprice may choose. Before they have been married a year he learns that excitement is the breath of life to her—that she must have new experiences, new friends, new sensations. He gets alarmed as he realizes that the fault is not in the girl as much as in what is back of her—in the temperament of her mother, who had only one redeeming quality, and in the temperament of her unknown father, who quite possibly had not one. He begins to feel that he has married a victim of heredity. Not all the care in her bringing-up, not all the years in that quiet convent, have eradicated the scarlet germs of her parentage. Sometimes he sees the devil himself look out of the eyes he loves."

"That's good," said the Author. "Go ahead."

"Picture her gradual reversion to hereditary types," continued the secretary. "At first only mild bohemianism, little parties, a little champagne. Later larger parties and more champagne. Of course he does what he can, but he sees the impotence of moral suasion in the face of her native trend. He discovers that she deceives him and lies to him. He cannot let her go to these things alone, but he sees that she and her friends are openly bored by his presence. If you want a few strong touches of mental agony in your tale, write of him—tell what he goes through in these awful nights and days, these hideous weeks and months and years. His friends fall away from him because he will not fall away from his wife. They think he is willingly, viciously sharing this life which he loathes. Given all this, any one can see that the moment comes when he could not, in self-respect, have any relations with her. The mother, lost through love, retained in her fall the beauty of womanly tenderness and noble sacrifice. The daughter has no redeeming trait. He settles money on her—what little they had left—and leaves her. Could he write of these things to her mother? Here is a reason for his breaking his promise.

"From time to time he hears of her—always as the centre of some new and characteristically horrible bit of devilishness. As her money goes, and the pace begins to tell, let her drift from Paris to Vienna, to Budapest, to Berlin, to London, and back again to Paris, blazing a trail of scandal as she goes. She has the one decent impulse of dropping his name. But he knows the assumed one she trails through the filth of Europe.

"Back in Paris the Lily disports a [illegible] at the Jardin de Paris and later in [illegible] coarser whirl of the Moulin Rouge. [illegible] him see her there some night, when h[illegible] taking a party of English friends thro[illegible] it on a sight-seeing expedition. T[illegible] can be an English girl in the part[illegible] sweet woman who has no right to be [illegible] even on that innocent little tour of[illegible] spection. She is on his arm, and he [illegible] glad to feel her leaning on him. A ma[illegible] may love twice, and the ruin of his first may lend strength to his second love. They stop to look at the dancing; one doesn't want to look at it long, even if he is a man and hasn't a good woman with him. Suddenly something twitches his other arm—a hideous thing, all skin and bone and paint and fever, and cheap, ghastly finery. It is his wife. She smirks at him like the lost soul she is. He recoils so that her brazen shame feels it and she drifts back into the crowd. The English woman recoils from him. Shall we say that she was in love with him? Perhaps she was, but she got over it when she saw ɔok of understanding between those ıat told of a past."

m-m," murmured the Author, doubt-

wo weeks later, a letter comes one ing, badly written, smelling of cheap and grimy about the edges. It ıim his wife is ill at a given address e *Quartier,* and it is signed with a ıe he doesn't know. He goes there l finds her. She is not in such straits s you said her mother was. Her woman riends are doing what they can for her. The room is clean and she has actual necessities. It may be some comfort to her, however, to have him take charge of her. He gets another doctor and a nurse, and he rents a room across the hall to be within reach. He spends most of his time there, and she takes it quite as a matter of course that he should. She never speaks of the past, and an odd sort of new life begins between them, in that little room where she lies dying. He reads to her a good deal, and she seems to like to have him around. When other

men come to inquire how she is the
sent away, but when women com
says, 'Let them come in and learn
thing from it if they can.' They
but I doubt if they learn much.
have seen it all too often before. H
the doctor and nurse are the only
with her at the last, and it is just as

"Late one afternoon he is standin
the window of her room looking out, wh
the nurse calls him. He goes to the be
and his wife motions to him to take he
hand. He sits down and holds it. He knows at once that she is dying. She looks up at him with an expression in her eyes that he had seen sometimes in those first weeks in Spain, years ago—the expression they took on when she had hurt him and was sorry. He had never seen it since then, until this afternoon. She signs to him to bend over her.

"'You are good,' she says. 'I am sorry I ruined your life—and my own. But you never understood me. No man could. Only one person in the world might have saved me—my mother. If

ıd lived, and been with me so I could
: pureness and her faith in me, I
should have lived and died a good
'.'

dying faith in Madame Fleury
ınds, you see, to her mother's
In all the horrible lessons of those
ng years she had never learned
spect her mother. She died an hour
."

The secretary stopped abruptly; he seemed unconscious of the sudden change of tense in his last sentence. He seemed also unconscious of the presence of his employer, who had drawn his note-book from his pocket and was turning the leaves, flushing darkly as he did so. As the other lapsed into silence, the Author spoke impulsively.

"Forgive me," he said. "It was stupid of me not to have recalled your name. Life writes stranger stories than fiction dares. I must have hurt you, but it was unconsciously, you know." He offered his hand, which *The* Young Man grasped in silence.

The Author hesitated a moment. His lips were set, but there was a softer expression in his eyes and he spoke with perfect simplicity and feeling.

"Of course," he said, "I shall not write the story. But you may imagine how deeply I feel your end of it when I tell you I might have played your rôle, only that Madame Fleury found me—wanting!"

THE END

PZ
3
J763
T 5

53425

Jordan, Elizabeth Garver

Tales of destiny